Unforgettable

I0620249

Robert regretted giving Maddie the brandy…

Giggling, she raised her hand and pointed a manicured fingernail at him. "Do you know you have the same name as the famous playwright who writes those silly plays? His name is Robert Kendall, too. Why, you even *look* like him!" She gave her thigh a slap. "Hot damn! I'll bet people ask for your autograph, thinking you're him. And you sign 'em too, don'tcha, you sly little devil?"

Robert gave a low laugh. She was just too cute to resist. Playing along with her, he drawled, "Yup. I sign every one. That's because I really am him."

"No!" she giggled again.

Robert shook his head and smiled. "It's true. I am. I have no reason to lie."

"All men lie," she remarked dryly, her mind flashing back to that afternoon and Alex.

Robert picked up on it. "My guess is that you've been burned and badly. Who hasn't? Just don't judge me by someone else." He rose from his seat and turned the radio on. The haunting rendition of *Unforgettable* enveloped the room. The soul-wrenching duet by the late Nat King Cole and his daughter had been Alex's love song to her. Now he was gone, and the melody cut through Maddie like a knife…

Unforgettable

Lucille Naroian

Licensed and produced by
Penumbra Publishing
www.penumbrapublishing.com

PRINTED IN THE UNITED STATES OF AMERICA

Copyright © 2009 Lucille Naroian. All rights reserved.

ISBN/EAN13: 978-1-935563-04-4

~Author Acknowledgment~

To Dr. Christine Wenberg … without your help, none of this would be possible.

Unforgettable

by

Lucille Naroian

CHAPTER ONE

---

*H*ad Maddie Price been paying attention to her surroundings instead of driving recklessly at night in hot pursuit of Alex Bradford, she would have seen the caution lights on the side of the road, slowed down, and avoided the accident. But at that particular moment, Maddie was oblivious to everything. Not even the rain that fell in sheets was capable of putting a halt to her seemingly impossible quest. Therefore, when her Chevy's left front tire slammed into the crater-size pothole and blew out, Maddie was totally unprepared.

Instinctively she hit the brakes, sending the vehicle skidding across the washed-out double lane highway. For a spine-tingling minute the car spun out of control, then stopped on the muddy shoulder of the road.

When the erratic pounding of her heart finally quieted, she turned off the ignition and gave the steering wheel a frustrated whack.

"Damn you, Alex! It's all your fault!" she yelled, blaming him for causing another catastrophe to come her way. Truth was, she was solely to blame for this mess. Hell-bent on reaching him, she defiantly set out from Boston to Provincetown in a blustering rain storm that was rapidly sweeping up the Eastern seacoast. Fully aware that the

1

major arteries leading south to Cape Cod were flooded, she unwisely disregarded the weatherman's warning to keep off the roads.

Under ordinary circumstances, Maddie would have waited. But time was not on her side. It was imperative she reach Alex tonight ... before dawn ... before he boarded that plane to Paris.

Just thinking about it brought a lump to Maddie's throat. *I can't let that happen*, she told herself, her fury mounting.

With a determined hand, she twisted the key in the ignition and willed the car to move. When the battered tire thumped and sank deeper into the mud, Maddie let out a defeated sob. What was she going to do now? There wasn't a gas station in sight, and even though she wasn't marooned on some desolate road, at this particular stretch she couldn't see any signs of civilization.

Slumping down into the seat, she tried to relax and come up with a viable solution. That's when she remembered catching a glimpse of a large beach house on the right about five minutes earlier. Its stately elegance had somehow caught her eye, and she'd noticed, through the rivulets streaming down the side window, a faint ray of light filtering from one of its windows.

A wave of relief swept over her. Someone was nearby. Hope was not lost after all.

She tucked the tapered legs of her jeans into her brown leather boots, and decided to walk back to the house, ignoring the fact that such a trek could put her into a situation more perilous than thc one she was in now. Nevertheless, it was a chance she had to take.

With her purse tucked under her arm, she reached for

the door handle. Just as she touched it, a jagged streak of lightening split the sky. A violent gust of wind rocked her small car. Sheer terror gripped her as she waited for the car to still. When it finally did, she reconsidered the danger and abandoned her attempt to seek help.

Gazing forlornly out the rain-drenched window, she considered her options. Not a soul had passed by since she'd been there, and it was doubtful that anyone would. Therefore, option one was to stay put and wait out the storm. Mulling it over, she decided that choice was out of the question. The idea of spending the night in an impotent vehicle sent shivers along her spine.

What if the storm developed into a hurricane? She'd have no chance of survival in her old Chevy. The car was too light-weight to guarantee her safety. Therefore, option two was her only choice. She'd have to change the tire herself. It didn't matter that she'd never attempted to change a tire before. The fact was, it had to be done.

Resigned to her fate, she took a deep breath and accepted the challenge. With a not so steady hand, she removed the key from the ignition, tied a silk scarf around her coiled, honey blonde hair, and turned up the collar on her navy pea jacket.

Moving quickly, she reached over to the glove compartment and withdrew a dented yellow flashlight. She couldn't remember the last time she'd used the old thing, and was certain that by now the batteries were dead. Holding her breath, she switched it on. A bright beam of light spread across the seat. Maddie smiled. Something had finally gone right. She switched off the light, pushed open the door, and carefully stepped out.

To her horror, the water on the road reached to the

top of her boots. Worse yet, the pothole had practically swallowed the useless tire completely. Emitting a groan, she squinted her eyes against the driving rain and crouched down beside the fender to inspect the damage, wondering how she was going to wedge a jack under a bumper she could barely see, and on solid ground when there was none. Her worries went into overdrive. What if the damage went beyond the tire? What if the axle or frame was broken? If that were the case, she'd have to total the car because the cost of repairs would far exceed what the old clunker was worth.

Suddenly, Maddie shook her head and stood upright, refusing to give in to another negative thought. It was simply tire trouble, she told herself, and nothing more. And if she was ever going to reach Alex tonight, she'd better get moving.

Pulling the jacket collar tighter around her neck, she turned and waded to the rear of the car. Just as she reached the trunk, she heard a sound. Hesitating a moment, she scanned the washed-out road, the stretch of isolated beach, then the sides and rear of the car, but saw nothing. Her imagination was playing tricks on her, she decided, as she shrugged her shoulders and slid the trunk key into the lock.

No sooner did it click when she heard the sound again. Switching on the flashlight, she aimed it in the direction of the noise. What she saw turned her insides to jelly.

Coming at her with lightening speed was the largest Doberman Pinscher she had ever seen. Black as the night, it charged through the murky water, its glassy eyes and sharp pointed teeth well illuminated by the lightening.

Unable to move, Maddie heard a sob leave her

4

throat, and her knees went weak as she realized in a moment she would become the victim of this deadly creature.

With only the thin flashlight for protection, she clutched it tightly, crossed her arms against her chest, and dug her chin deep into her jacket collar. It was all just too much! Standing beside a useless hunk of junk with that hellhound charging toward her, she vowed that if she lived through this, she would get even with Alex one way or another.

The dog, just inches away, focused its eyes intently on her. When she heard the beast's low, throaty growl, she flung the flashlight in its path and somehow found the strength to run. It was a mistake she soon regretted. As if fired from a cannon, the dog shot up on its hind legs and pounced its huge paws onto Maddie's shoulders, pinning her to the side of the car. She could actually feel the heat of its breath on her throat as it opened its jaws wider.

A wave of dizziness came over her, and for a moment she prayed she *would* faint. Unable to face her fate, with the attack-dog snarling at her throat, she shut her eyes tight. Her only thought now was that she didn't want to die ... not here ... not like this.

What Maddie needed was a miracle, and it came, just in time, in the form of a pickup truck that screeched to a halt beside her. Because of the howling wind, she didn't hear the driver's door slam, but she did hear a piercing whistle, and that's when her eyes flew open. The animal responded immediately to the sound and mercifully slid its heavy claw-tipped paws from Maddie's trembling shoulders. Immediately she felt a different pressure replacing the dog's paws – a pair of strong, yet comforting hands.

Maddie's eyes lifted to meet the stranger's shadowed

face. When he spoke, his voice was gentle with seeming genuine concern. "Are you hurt?"

"N-no," she stammered with a sigh of relief as she wiped the stream of tears and rain from her eyes. "B-but the dog. Please get him away from me!"

The stranger pulled the hood of his slicker further down to shield his face from the pounding rain. "Don't be afraid, Miss!" he shouted. "He belongs to me. I'm real sorry he frightened you."

Immediately anger replaced her fear. "Frighten me!" she snapped. "He was ready to tear out my throat! How dare you let something like that run loose? He belongs on a leash. Better yet, in a cage!"

The man stiffened. "I never let Caesar run loose. He got away from me when I went outside to lock the gate. Hard to believe, but he's never done this before. He must have sensed there was trouble up the road, and apparently he was right." The man reached down and patted the dog, who now stood still beside his master. Turning, the animal jumped onto the open back of the truck.

The man took a step backwards, reached into the pocket of his slicker, and took out a long silver flashlight. Switching it on, he gave the Chevy the once over. "What's wrong with your car?"

Maddie's shoulders sagged both from embarrassment and utter helplessness. "I'm afraid I wasn't paying attention and hit something hard in the road!" she shouted, trying to be heard above the wind. "It wrecked my tire."

"Must have been that damn pothole!" he shouted back. "Didn't you see the warning sign?"

"What warning sign?"

"Back there on that pole," he answered, pointing in

6

its direction. "There's a sign and a set of bright yellow caution lights. Even in this rain, you couldn't have missed them."

She could barely make out what he was saying as he waded off to inspect the battered tire. Centering the light on the tattered wheel, he remarked, "You must have been going like a bat out of hell!"

"Never mind that!" she snapped. "The important thing is, can you fix it for me? I have a spare in the trunk."

He turned the flashlight on her angry face. "No way, Miss."

"Please, Mister," she begged. "I just have to get to Provincetown tonight!"

The stranger switched off the light and returned it to his pocket. "The tire's wedged too deeply in the mud. Looks like your car is going to have to sit here until the storm ends."

"I can't wait that long!" she shouted, blinking her eyes rapidly against the rain. "Didn't you hear me? I've got to get there tonight!"

The man became impatient. "I heard you perfectly, Miss, but again, I can't help you. Not tonight, anyway."

Maddie sighed and thought a minute. "What about a gas station? Isn't there one around here somewhere?"

"Sure," he yelled. "There's one just around the bend. But it's closed because of the storm. Sorry, but you're just going to have to wait till tomorrow."

"Tomorrow's too late!" she gasped. Balling her fists in frustration, she turned quickly and began trudging towards the driver's side of the car.

The stranger caught her by the arm. "Why is tomorrow too late?" he asked. "Is there a family

7

emergency?"

"No, there's no family emergency," she replied, harshly. She was not about to admit she had risked life and limb in a futile attempt to stop a man from leaving her. She turned her face away and said forlornly, "I'll just stay here for the night."

The man eyed her closely and said in disbelief, "You don't really plan to spend the night in this wreck!"

"Yes, I do," she answered, feeling absolutely sick inside.

"That's crazy!" he said, his patience obviously wearing thin. "My place is about three hundred yards back down the road. You're welcome to stay the night. It's better than being alone out here. At least you'll be dry ... and safe."

And safe. It was strange the way he had tagged on that last phrase. She understood he had paused purposely for effect.

As if capable of reading her thoughts, the man gave her a reassuring smile. "Look, I can understand your apprehension. If I were a woman in this predicament, I'd be leery of going off with a stranger myself. But, it's your choice."

Looking up at him, Maddie replied in an equally placating tone, "Thanks. I appreciate the offer."

He gave her a quick smile. "So, what do you say? And make it quick before we both catch pneumonia."

No sooner had he asked the question when a streak of lightening struck a tree stump on the opposite side of the road, splitting it in two. It was all Maddie needed. "Yes."

* * * * *

Settling herself beside the stranger in his warm truck,

Maddie got a closer look at him as he pushed back the hood on his slicker and threaded long fingers through his thick, dark hair. The sight of his handsome profile etched against the intermittent flashes of lightening brought an unexpected flush to her cheeks. She pressed her icy cold palms against her face, hoping he hadn't noticed, but he had.

Patting her gently on her arm, he said reassuringly, "Relax. Everything will turn out okay." Maddie knew he was trying to banish her fear. But what she was feeling was anything *but* fear. Sitting there so close to him, she felt the flutter of butterflies in the pit of her stomach. Swallowing hard, she managed to lie with some degree of conviction. "I'm not nervous. Just hot one minute, cold the next."

"A shot of brandy will take care of that," he replied as he removed his hand and started the engine.

Confused by her emotional response to his nearness and touch, Maddie sat back and tried to relax, but when she glanced at her disabled car, she became deeply depressed. Even if the storm ended by dawn as expected, and she was able to get help from one of the garages in town, it would be too late to reach Alex. Tears of despair brimmed her eyes, so she shut them tightly to hold them back. She remained lost in her melancholy until the stranger stopped the truck and turned off the engine.

Opening her eyes, she peered out the window and grinned, thinking it ironic that this rambling house was the one she'd tried to reach earlier.

After drawing the hood back onto his head, Maddie's companion got out of the truck, then closing the door behind him, summoned his dog with a loud whistle. Fast on his master's heels, the beast began running in circles, visibly happy to be home.

Odd, but Maddie felt the same as she followed closely behind and inspected the full exterior of the house. Flanking the crushed sea shell driveway was a low stone wall shrouded with leaves deposited by the storm from the belt of trees that formed a semi-circle around the house. Wide brick steps led to a white over-sized paneled door. Centered between the panels was a brass plate on which the name Kendall was inscribed.

Maddie turned to him and asked, "Are you *Mr.* Kendall?"

"In the flesh," he quipped. "But please, call me Robert. And you?"

"Madelyn Price," she answered softly. "But everyone calls me Maddie."

"Nice to meet you, Maddie," he returned. "Welcome to my humble abode."

After exchanging amenities, Robert inserted the key in the lock, then thrust open the door and gestured Maddie inside. When all three had entered the narrow foyer, the dog placed himself in front of her, gave a low throaty growl, and raised his proud head in protest to her admittance. Continuing to growl, he bared his sharp, white teeth. Instinctively Maddie jumped back and brought the heel of her boot firmly down on the toe of Robert's boot. When he let out a painful howl, Maddie quickly jumped forward. Pivoting around, she came face to face with the tall, handsome Robert Kendall.

Although the foyer was dimly lit, they could clearly see each other's face. For a moment their eyes met and locked, sending a disquieting shiver racing through Maddie's already shivering body.

Finally she came to her senses. "E-excuse me," she

stammered, blushing profusely.

"No harm done." He smiled, gazing down at her face as he removed his rain-streaked slicker. He then held out his hand for her jacket and scarf. Caesar continued to growl in protest. This time the man turned to the dog and commanded, "Enough!" Maddie was impressed to find that one word was all it took to quiet the animal, who turned and sauntered towards the fireplace.

Grateful to be rid of her sopping wet coverings, Maddie quickly handed them to Robert, who draped them over a ladder-back chair near the fire.

Stepping quickly to the closet in the hall, he opened the door and deposited his slicker inside. After closing it, he placed his hands on his hips and gazed directly into her wide aquamarine eyes. A smile played gently on his lips. "Now for those wet clothes," he practically whispered, savoring the way her V-neck sweater clung to her full rounded breasts with their peaks pointed straight at him.

Her skin tight jeans were molded to her slim hips and long shapely legs causing the muscles in his jaw to tighten. *God, she's incredible*, he thought, then mentally shook himself from the direction his thoughts were taking him.

Maddie stood there like a mannequin, unable to move under his intimate stare, but her mind was racing a mile a minute. She knew what he was thinking, and for some inexplicable reason, she welcomed the intimate gaze. It brought an immediate flush to her cheeks. Suddenly, she remembered that they had forgotten her luggage in the trunk of her car.

"My suitcases!" she gasped. "How could I have forgotten them? Everything I–"

"Relax. I'll go back and get them," he said tightly, trying not to reveal his displeasure. Right now, the last thing in the world he wanted to do was take his eyes off her incredible body and trudge back out into the storm. But he had no choice, he told himself. After all, if he was going to play a knight-in-shining-armor, he had to take the bad with the good. Heaving a sigh, he pointed at Maddie and ordered, "Don't move."

Now what? She wondered, wrapping her arms around herself. She was freezing and he had to know it. So, why wasn't he leading her to the fireplace to warm herself? And where was he going, she wondered as he went around the fireplace and disappeared.

He was back in seconds, holding a towel and a blue terry cloth robe, which, from the looks of its size, was definitely his, and a pair of terry cloth slippers to match.

"Here, dry off and put these on." He pushed the items into her trembling hands. "You can put your wet things in the dryer in the mud room which is right across from you. Those jeans will take forever to dry in front of the fire." Then, like a game show contestant who was trying to beat the clock or lose the prize, he flung open the closet door, grabbed his slicker, and went over to the dog. "You," he snapped at the animal, who looked back at him with a raised eyebrow, "don't you dare move! Understand?"

The dog raised the other brow at the command. His master rarely left the house without him. Caesar's gaze turned to Maddie. So did Robert's.

"Where are your keys?"

"In my purse on the chair. And thank y–"

"No problem," he stated flatly. He opened the purse, grabbed the keys, and slammed the door behind him.

* * * * *

"Nice doggie," Maddie said in a quivering voice, striving to remain calm as she stepped cautiously to the fire. The dog's ominous stare followed her every move, increasing her nervousness. She didn't trust the beast. Not for a minute.

As their eyes locked, she sucked in a deep, unsteady breath and slowly removed her boots. Her heart hammered wildly against her chest as she began to remove her sweater. Even when it dropped to the floor, the dog's eyes never left hers. Becoming increasingly agitated, she wanted to tell the animal to stop looking at her *that* way.

"Now I know why they call dogs man's best friend," she stated, glaring back at him. "Men and dogs relate perfectly. A female is a female whether she has two legs or four."

Still peering at him out of the corner of her eye, she removed the pins from her hair and set them on the mantle. After wiping her face dry with the towel, she pushed her hair forward, then twisted the towel around it turban style.

Praying she'd be in the robe before Robert returned, she quickly unzipped her jeans, hooked her thumbs into the waistbands of both the jeans and panties, and began inching them down her legs.

"You could at least have the decency to turn your head!" she snapped, standing totally naked before the gazing beast.

"Why should he? He has good taste, just like his master."

CHAPTER TWO

"How long have you been standing there?" Maddie gasped, fixing her unbelieving eyes squarely on him as she snatched up the robe that was draped over the chair by the fireplace.

"Sorry I startled you," he said. He knew he should have looked away, but he couldn't. Unhurriedly, he let his eyes travel over her body, taking in every detail of her luscious curves.

"Sorry, my foot," she mumbled under her breath. She might have believed him if his lips weren't curved in a half-smile, or his dark eyes not glazed with desire. He was enjoying every minute of her embarrassment. Spinning on her heels, she quickly turned her back to him and pulled on the soft, fluffy garment.

This had to be the worst day of her life, she told herself, tying a knot in the robe's belt. So far, it appeared tonight was turning out to be pretty good for him.

"No matter what you believe," he said, heading for the hall closet, "I wasn't ogling you like some pervert. I'm a normal guy who appreciates a beautiful woman. I was also enjoying your one-sided conversation with Caesar. Nevertheless, please forgive my bad manners. I didn't think I had to knock on my own door first."

14

Depositing his slicker and her luggage in the closet, he gently closed the door and came to her side. "Can we put this little episode behind us and get on with it?"

Maddie frowned. "Get on with what?"

"The brandy," he answered. "Remember? Or did *you* have something else in mind?" He wiggled his eyebrows and tapped on an imaginary cigar near his mouth like Groucho Marx.

It was a bad imitation, but effective enough to change Maddie's anger to a hearty laugh. He had a wonderful sense of humor, something Alex definitely lacked. *Alex*. The thought of him suddenly put an end to her smile.

"So, how do you like this room?" Robert asked proudly. "I decorated it myself."

She gazed around at his handiwork. As wide as it was long, the room was magnificently impressive with a high, natural beamed ceiling and a definite masculine décor. Dominating its vastness was an enormous brown corduroy sofa flanked by square pinewood tables on which set two ginger jar lamps that spread a soft golden glow on the polished hardwood floor and multicolored braided rug.

To the right of the sofa was a tan corded over-stuffed chair that had seen better days. Behind it stood wide, rustic-looking book cases crammed with books and magazines, and a small statuette, which Maddie guessed to be an award of some sort. But the feature that captivated her the most was the floor-to-ceiling field stone fireplace. It's warm, crackling flames drew her like a magnet.

Sensing her delight in the room's hominess, Robert offered her a seat by the fire. Without hesitating, Maddie went to the sofa and curled up in a corner on the soft cushions. Glancing over to the dog, Maddie noticed the beast continued to stare at her intently, but when his master lowered his large frame into the corded chair opposite her, the animal slid his head onto his paws and went to sleep.

"Now for that brandy and some soothing music." Turning sideways to a glass tea cart beside the chair, he reached down to the bottom shelf that held a small compact stereo. With a push of a button, the room was immediately filled with what she could only describe as *Music for Lovers.* After adjusting the volume, Robert reached above and filled two brandy snifters with amber-colored liquid. As he handed a glass to her, their finger tips touched, sending sparks of recognition through her. She saw his eyes flicker and knew he felt it too.

Trying to feign indifference, she nevertheless felt an involuntary blush heat her cheeks. Lowering her gaze to her lap, she raised the glass to her lips and sipped slowly.

"Feeling better?" he asked after swallowing a large portion of his brandy.

Maddie nodded, "Much, thank you, Mr. Kendall."

"It's Robert, remember?" he reminded her, his dark eyes never leaving her face.

Oh, yes. Sorry … Robert." Immediately her eyes focused on his full, sensuous mouth.

Realizing where her eyes were trained, Robert playfully teased her by biting his lower lip ever so lightly. The color in her cheeks deepened. His body hardened in instant reaction to her, and he made no effort to hide it, but rather gave her a tantalizing smile.

When Maddie found herself reciprocating with a tentative smile of her own, a tiny voice in the back of her mind warned her that flirting with a total stranger was treading on dangerous ground, and if she wasn't careful, she might find herself in a situation she might not be able to control.

For some crazy reason, she ignored her inner voice. Smiling boldly at his handsome face, she took a gulp of the rich, smooth brandy. Immediately, the liquor rushed to her head, making her feel even warmer and just a tiny bit giddy.

Giggling outright, she raised her free hand and shook a manicured fingernail at him. "Do you realize that you have the same name as the famous playwright who writes those silly plays? His name is Robert Kendall, too. Why, you even *look* like him!" She gave her thigh a slap. "Hot damn! I'll bet people even ask you for your autograph, thinking you're him. And you sign 'em too, don't you, you sly little devil?"

Robert gave a low laugh. She was just too cute to resist. Playing along with her, he drawled, "Yup. I sign everyone. That's because I really *am* him."

"No!" she giggled again.

Robert shook his head and smiled. "Yes, I am. I could *never* lie to a cute little tipsy blonde named Maddie, or to anyone else, for that matter."

"Really?' she remarked, taking another healthy sip of brandy. "Then prove it."

"Be glad to." Rising from his seat, he began to regret having given her a drink in the first place. It was quite apparent she couldn't hold her liquor very well.

Walking to the bookcase behind her, he gently picked up the statuette – his most prized possession – and set it on the coffee table in front of her. "There," he said proudly, taking his seat again. "Do you know what that is?"

She looked at it through blurry eyes and said, "Sure I do. It's a bowling trophy. My father had one just li–"

"I don't think so," Robert interrupted, shaking his head in amusement. "It's called a Tony award. I got it three years ago for my play, *The China Doll*. It ran on Broadway for almost two years. You didn't happen to catch it, did you?"

"Sorry," she apologized, lowering her eyes to her drink. "I've never been to a play on Broadway. But now that you mention it, I remember reading about it in the entertainment section of the *Boston Globe*. The critics loved it." She turned her head, hoping he couldn't see how suddenly embarrassed she was, then whispered, "I apologize for doubting you and for calling your beautiful award a bowling trophy. I feel really stupid."

Robert winced, wondering what gem was about to come out of her mouth next.

She swallowed the last of her brandy. Trying to recapture some of her dignity, she raised her chin and said, "I'm sure that you and *Mrs.* Kendall must be so proud."

"There is no Mrs. Kendall. I'm a widower." He didn't mean to sound hard-hearted. The words just came out that way. He didn't want to talk about his late wife and hoped Maddie would leave the subject alone. She did, but that didn't stop him from asking about *her* marital status.

Leaning forward, he rested his elbows on his thighs and bluntly asked, "Is there a *Mr.* Price?"

No sooner had he posed the question when the haunting rendition of *Unforgettable* enveloped the room. The soul-wrenching duet by the late Nat King Cole and his daughter had been Alex's love song to her. They had danced to it on their very first date, and she vividly remembered how it played softly in the background the night they had made love together for the first time. Now the melody cut through Maddie like a knife, and suddenly all the coy playfulness went out of her.

She sat stiff and glassy-eyed as her mind raced back to the chapel where, just hours before, she and Alex were to be married. But he had never showed up. Perplexed, she had borrowed the minister's phone in his study and called his apartment, but all she got was a busy signal. A second call to the telephone company assured her that nothing was wrong. The phone was simply off the hook.

From his seat nearby, Robert watched confused, as an odd look of pain crossed Maddie's lovely face. Caesar lifted his head with a small whine, awaking from his nap in front of the fire, as if sensing something was wrong. Robert barely noticed as his dog slinked out of the room to find a more restful place to nap. Focusing on Maddie, he frowned, trying to determine what was going through her mind at that moment.

The horrendous fact that she had been conned registered so clearly in Maddie's consciousness, it dragged a devastating sob from her throat. Completely out of control now, she lowered her face to her hands and cried bitterly.

Stunned by her sudden emotional outburst, Robert froze. But, when he realized she was fast on the verge of hysterics, he quickly rose from his seat, sat down beside her and gathered her up into his strong, powerful arms. For a long while he sat there rocking her gently, offering her comfort – from what, he had no idea.

When finally there were no more tears to shed, Maddie pulled back, her embarrassment equal to her pain. "Oh God, I-I'm so sorry," she mumbled, looking away in utter humiliation. She was so overcome with shame at having lost all self-control, she wished she could magically vanish.

Her distress moved Robert deeply. He took a handkerchief from his jeans pocket and began wiping the tears from her cheeks. Cupping her quivering chin in his palm, he turned her face back to his and said softly, "I'm sorry for upsetting you. I just came to the conclusion that there *is* a Mr. Price and he's either–"

"His name isn't Price," she grumbled, sniffling. "It's Bradford. Alex Bradford."

"I don't understand…"

"A-at first I didn't either," she slurred, her throat still thick from her tears. "But, now I do. We were supposed to be married this afternoon, but he never showed up. Do you know how humiliating that is?"

"Maybe he's been in an accident," Robert offered.

"No," she said with a heavy sigh, fighting hard to hold back another round of tears. "Trust me. He just wanted out."

Finding himself at a loss for words, Robert took his hand from her chin, rose from the sofa, and walked over to the cart where he poured himself another brandy. Swallowing a healthy amount, he turned to her and asked almost angrily, "Is he the reason you were out in this storm?"

"Yes," she admitted, burrowing deeper into the cushions. "I was on my way to his apartment."

"Why?" he asked, swallowing the last of his drink.

"To get back what's mine. But if I don't get there in time, he'll be gone. It'll all be gone."

Robert shook his head in disbelief. "You mean to tell me you risked your life in this storm just to get back some personal belongings?" He sat beside her on the couch.

His harsh, insensitive question caught her off guard. Turning towards him, her eyes flinty with anger, she shouted, "He stole *everything* from me! And he's not going to get away with it! I won't let him!"

"You're going to have to," he stated flatly, "because right now there is absolutely nothing you can do about it."

No sooner were the words spoken when Maddie jumped to her feet. "Nothing, huh?" she spat out. "Where's your phone? I'll find someway to get to him!"

Taking into consideration her fierce determination, Robert backed off. What was the point of trying to reason with her? Obviously her anger was out of control, and anything he had to say would fall on deaf ears. So why should he give a damn what she did? Why should he care?

Because she was someone in deep pain, that's why, he told himself. Pain that he could relate to easily. Not that long ago, he had been where she was now, emotionally. And there had been no one to give *him* comfort ...show *him* compassion. And, most of all, bring *him* to his senses. No one ... until a young man named Andy came into his life.

On that momentous day, Robert was auditioning unknowns for the play he was writing. Just as the last actor finished up his lines, the back door to the rented studio flew open, and a high-pitched voice with a thick southern accent drawled, "Hol' on thar, Mista Kendall! Ah'm the acta you been lookin' fer. Ah'da gotten here soonah, but ma parol' offissa wanted a secon' helpin' o' grits!"

For the first time in a long time, Robert laughed till the tears flowed. When he was finally able to stop, he took a seat in the back of the studio and listened in awe while Andy read a few lines. The character was a French waiter, and by the time he had completed the third sentence, Robert swore that the young man had just stepped off the plane from Paris.

From that day on, Andy had become Robert's best friend. And, as best friends often sense such things, Andy realized that for some reason Robert was deeply troubled.

Not wanting to intrude on Robert's privacy, Andy asked no questions, but waited patiently for his friend to open up to him. And Robert did – late one night in a bar in Woods Hole, after one too many drinks. When he was through, Robert asked for his friend's advice. His companion spoke straight from the hip, without reservation or hesitation, knowing full well that his advice was not what Robert wanted to hear. In fact, Andy considered it might even put an end to their friendship. But the bottom line was that Robert needed to be brought to his senses in order to get on with his life.

Which was exactly what Maddie needed now...a genuine friend to bring her to her senses.

With one swift motion, Robert caught her by the arm and pulled her back down beside him. "I know you're furious with me, and you don't want to listen, but consider this. For Alex to do what he did, what makes you think he'll see you? Even if you do reach him tonight?"

Maddie looked him in the eyes. "Oh, he'll see me," she snapped, then flashed Robert a wicked smile. "I'll see to it he does."

Robert became incensed. "Get real, girl, and face the truth. The guy's a con artist. He stole from you. He took what he wanted, and it wasn't you. So now he's gone. Let him go. Because if he has to physically hurt you to get you away from him, he just might. Then what? Is what he took worth risking your life? For your own sake, don't take any more foolish chances. I know you're hurting. But let him go and be glad that he's gone and that you're okay."

"I can't, I just can't!" she spat out. Robert could see in her fiery blue eyes a volcanic fury – a fury that was about to erupt. And when it did, it came from the very depths of her soul.

"I can't just let him walk away Scott-free! He *owes* me – big time! I gave up my apartment and my job – *everything* – to marry him and move to Paris because I loved him and I believed him when he said he loved me, too.

"Look at me!" she bellowed, staring hard into Robert's eyes. "I'm thirty-one years old! I've spent my life working to support myself and my father, who did nothing but wallow in self-pity by drinking himself into oblivion trying to drown out the pain of my mother's death. I put my life aside for him, and when he died I vowed I'd never work to support a man again.

"Then Alex came along and swept me off my feet. Even though he was a dirt-poor artist, I knew he was good and believed one day he'd be successful. And to prove my love, I gave him everything, and he took it – including every cent I had.

"At dawn, he's leaving for Paris. He's chartered a private plane that's supposed to take us to a new life – a better life, and by God, Robert, if I have to *walk* to Provincetown tonight, I'll do it. I have to. He stole ten thousand dollars from my travel bag earlier today when he brought me to my friend's home to prepare for the wedding. When he didn't show up at the chapel, I knew ... I just knew that he'd taken the money. And I was right. When the wedding party returned to the house, I immediately checked my travel bag and found the money gone. Now can you understand why I'm determined to get to him?"

"Right now, I almost believe you could do it," Robert said, watching her closely as she slumped against the back of the couch, her fury spent.

Sighing deeply, she said, "If you knew me better, you wouldn't doubt it for a minute."

Trying to fight the impulse to take her back into his caress, Robert lifted his arm and draped it behind her. "Then give *me* a chance to know you better," he murmured huskily, his dark eyes sweeping over her small, delicate features.

Maddie sneered at him coldly. "Haven't you heard a word I've said?"

"I heard every word," he answered, nodding his head. "My question is, didn't you hear yourself?"

Infuriated with him, she moved her mouth to speak, but he silenced her by pressing a finger gently against her lips. "You're angry and hurt. That's understandable. The guy's a bastard for what he did. But, the truth is that right now you want him *not* because you love him, but because your ego and wallet have suffered a helluva blow. So you've got all the right in the world to want his head on a platter. What bothers me is that you told him ... I just *know* you did, that you had that kind of cash stashed away *before* he popped the question. Am I right?"

She nodded her head.

"Figures," he continued. "Therefore, he also knew you'd have it with you if you were going to leave right after the wedding. Right?"

Shoving his hand away from her mouth, she snarled, "Yes. And, I know where this interrogation is headed. I should've had the money converted to traveler's checks, or even had a cashier's check made out to me. But I didn't. I didn't want the hassle of exchanging checks to francs. So now I'm paying the price for not covering my butt. At the time, I didn't think I had to. I loved the guy and trusted him. And now, for the life of me, I just can't get it through my thick head that he didn't love me, that … that he was marrying me just for my money. I mean, we're not talking millions here, Robert."

"That's because you're choosing to delude yourself, Maddie, and I can relate to that perfectly." he admitted dryly, remembering how he had deluded himself into believing that his late wife's irrational behavior was merely the result of stress. He had begged her repeatedly to seek professional help, but she wouldn't hear of it. And in the end, unable to cope with her own mood swings and self-destructiveness any longer, she took her own life.

Although he hid it well, Robert was deeply wounded by her death. For months he threw himself into his work, writing from dusk to dawn. Occasionally, he was obligated to attend social functions, and not wanting to be the topic of tabloid gossip by either showing up alone or with Andy, he would seek the company of actresses from his own theater group. But it never went further than that.

Not that women didn't try to gain his affections for the night. He was constantly being pursued … even propositioned. Admittedly, there were several occasions where he almost succumbed, but at the last minute he realized the potential danger, and backed off. Risky business, he called it. All the way around.

However, celibacy certainly didn't help his disposition either, as Andy had so clearly pointed out one rainy afternoon during a punishing game of racquetball.

"Man, you gotta get yourself a woman, and soon!" Andy cried out in pain when Robert sliced the ball, hitting his friend hard on his shin. "Get rid of some of that tension. 'Cause if you don't, they're gonna take me outa here in a wheelchair. It's time you let go of your hurt and guilt, and found yourself a good woman. She's out there somewhere. Trust me."

Thinking back on that day, Robert was convinced that Andy was either a helluva fortune teller or his guardian angel. Either way, he was always right on the money.

Like now, for example. Here beside him was a woman whose life was parallel to his. Both had suffered deep emotional pain. Both had the ability to love deeply and selflessly. What intrigued him more than her beauty, more than her feistiness, was that she touched a chord somewhere deep inside him. He could feel himself being drawn to her uncontrollably.

Perhaps, she was the woman Andy meant ... the woman who was destined for him. True, she was stubborn and defiant, yet she was also fragile and vulnerable. And, although she was not aware of it, she was fast becoming in his eyes the woman who had what it took to chip away at the wall he had built around himself and hidden behind for too long. The realization widened his eyes and brought a smile to his lips.

Maddie looked at him strangely. "Are you alright?" she asked. "You look like you've just witnessed the second coming."

God, if she only knew, he thought, deliberately moving his body closer to hers.

His clean male smell filled her senses, and her breath quickened. Fighting to remain calm, she drew a deep unsteady breath and dropped her gaze to her hands. "Maybe you're right." she murmured, sighing heavily. "Maybe I've been kidding myself all along."

"I wouldn't steer you wrong, Maddie," he whispered. Battling the hunger to feel her lips beneath his, he brazenly slid his mouth against her soft cheek.

His warm breath sent delicious chills through her body. She should have pushed him away, but she just couldn't. "Don't, Robert," she managed to get out. "You're confusing me."

Ever so slowly, his lips left her flushed cheek. He looked deeply into her eyes. "You couldn't feel confused if you were really in love with the guy," he said huskily. "That's the point *I* was trying to make."

"That's not fair," she said raggedly. "Maybe I've totally lost my mind, but I still want him."

"An hour ago ... maybe. Ten minutes ago ... maybe. But right now, you want me," he rasped, crushing her near-naked body against his. "And I want you. I know it's crazy, but from the moment we met, something magical happened between us. I feel it, and I know you do too. And, if you have any doubts about it, I'm going to clear them away right now."

Somewhere in the back of her brain, a voice screamed, *Run*! *Get away now*! But Maddie couldn't move. Wide-eyed and breathless with anticipation, she watched as he drew back, then slowly, very slowly, lowered his head to hers. When his hot, full lips closed over the softness of her mouth, she responded with a passion she never knew she possessed. From somewhere deep inside, a raw, animal-like hunger surfaced. Fused to him in a lengthy, searing kiss, she trembled uncontrollably. When his tongue rolled around hers, she wound her hands around his neck to pull him closer. She ached for release as his hard, vibrant body pressed against hers. His large hands moved possessively over her soft full breasts, then downward along her waist and hips, until finally they stopped and he squeezed her rounded bottom.

"Good God, Maddie..." he groaned, delighted but slightly awed by her fiery response. "I knew the minute I saw you I wanted you. Tell me that you want me, too."

A low moan escaped Maddie. "Oh, yes ... Alex ... yes."

CHAPTER THREE

*R*obert went stiff in her arms.

"Oh, God," Maddie groaned, realizing the terrible slip she had made. "I'm so sorry, Robert." Trying to save her dignity, she immediately changed her attitude and said hotly, "You had no right kissing me like that! You know my heart belongs to another man, and if you had any decency whatsoever, you'd–"

"Decency!" he cut in sharply, his mouth twisted in a contemptuous smirk. "Aren't you the pot calling the kettle black!"

"What's *that* supposed to mean?" she demanded in a cold rage.

Robert leveled himself slightly above her and growled, "Don't pull that innocent act on me! You wanted me to kiss you right from the start. You said so with your eyes ... with your body. And when I did, you didn't fight me, you kissed me back. Now, for a woman who's supposedly head over heels in love with another man, I'd hardly call your behavior decent, would you?"

He had her there, yet Maddie wouldn't give him the satisfaction of admitting he was right. She spat out defensively, "In my heart, I was kissing Alex!"

"The hell you were!" he hurled back in anger. "You

29

were kissing me!"

"Ooooh!" she seethed, planting her palms hard against his chest. "Believe what you want ... just get away from me."

Robert knew in his heart she didn't mean it, regardless of the icy tone of her voice. She wanted him as much as he wanted her, and no matter what it took, he was going to get her to admit it.

Instead of moving away, he raised his hand and stroked her cheek ever so softly. "Convince me it's Alex you want right now, and not me," he coaxed, "and I'll never come near you again."

There it was, the chance to say yes. He was giving her the out. All she had to do was take it.

Impatiently, Robert repeated his command. "Tell me you want *him*! Say it!"

"No, I can't." The words tore from Maddie's heart, and she closed her eyes against the shame of her confession. That she could love one man and want another with a passion so intense was beyond her understanding. Nevertheless, it was true. Robert knew it, and it was useless now for Maddie to deny it.

Slowly she opened her eyes and met Robert's. Without uttering a word, he covered her body with his. Once more his mouth sought hers, forcing her lips apart, his searing tongue rolling lazily over hers, driving her wild. She could feel his heart beating rapidly through the softness of her robe, and willingly she let her body mold to his in a soul-destroying kiss that seemed to go on forever, sending her senses spiraling.

When his hand slid inside the robe again to stroke the underside of her breast, she gasped at the burning ache it produced, and she wound her arms once again tightly around his neck. She knew she was inviting him to make love to her, but she couldn't help herself. She *wanted* him to go on kissing her, never to stop. She *wanted* to feel his hard, muscular body, now fully aroused, against hers. This time she was all too aware that the man loving her now was not Alex and, crazy as it was, she didn't care.

Keeping his lips pressed firmly on hers, Robert slid their bodies off the sofa, and with one swift motion, gathered her up in his arms. Taking long strides, he carried her up the staircase, stopping before a door that was slightly open.

With her head resting comfortably on his shoulder, Maddie waited breathlessly as they entered a semi-darkened room. Her heart skipped a beat when she heard him close the door behind them with the heel of his boot.

When he stopped by the side of the bed, he set her down on her feet. He cupped her radiant face in his hands and said huskily, "You don't have to do this if you really don't want to."

"I know," she said, breathing hard. "But I want to."

"Then undress me," he ordered softly.

Surprisingly, Maddie's fingers didn't tremble as she undid the buttons on his shirt, then returned slowly to rake through the mat of thick, dark hair on his chest. *Ah ... the feel of him ... so manly ... so virile...*

Rolling the shirt down his muscular arms, she watched it sail to the thick, carpeted floor. Robert wasted no time untying the belt on her robe. As it, too, fell to the floor, he reached up and removed the towel that held her long, blonde hair in place. The towel went flying, and her long blonde locks tumbled to the small of her back. Pulling her closer to him, he threaded his fingers into the thick, flowing curls.

"Robert ... Robert," she whispered, totally enthralled. Her need of him completely overtook her the moment her tender breasts made contact with his hard, furred chest.

"Give me your hands," he commanded, his voice barely a whisper. Clasping them to his, he lowered them to the belt on his jeans. Together, their hands worked quickly and expertly to remove all that remained, and when the last boot thumped softly to the carpet, Robert eased himself onto the cool sheets, pulling Maddie's body down onto his.

Was that thunder or the sound of her own heart pounding in her ears? She couldn't be sure. She had never experienced the feel of another man's naked body before except for Alex's, and even then their lovemaking had never brought her to such wantonness. But now, with her body covering Robert's, Maddie's newfound passion was aroused beyond her wildest imaginings. Boldly taking the initiative, she glided her lips along his shoulder to the side of his throat, growing giddy as she slowly made her way to his mouth.

Moaning in anticipation of what was to come, Robert parted his lips, then groaned aloud when at last her mouth swooped down hard on his. He kissed her fiercely, his limbs moving seductively beneath hers. With his fingertips, he drew tiny circles along the curve of her hips, waist, and sides of her breasts. His need for her overtaking him completely, he shifted her onto her back and raised himself slightly above her. Through the filmy white curtains that covered the French doors, the flashes of lightening from the raging storm momentarily illuminated the pale beauty of the woman Robert now had to have.

Her need matching his, Maddie slid her arms around his neck, straining her body against the hard length of his. When he couldn't wait a moment longer, he lowered himself down, entered her, then began to move in a slow, rocking motion.

Maddie felt herself being drawn deeper and deeper into a world she'd never encountered...a world where time stood still, and no one else existed but the two of them. Wanting him ... needing him desperately, she surrendered herself completely to him. He took her gently at first, then more fiercely as the violence of their lovemaking rose to a fevered pitch and exploded.

* * * * *

Maddie let out a deep sigh of contentment. "I never knew it could be this wonderful," she murmured, wrapping her arms even tighter around Robert. "I feel as if I died and went to heaven."

"That's what all you women say," he purred, nibbling at the fleshy part of her ear.

His words hit her like a splash of cold water, jolting her back to reality. Alex had been the only man she'd ever been with. But Robert ... how many women had shared his bed? From what he'd just said, Maddie surmised the count was high. Suddenly, terror overtook her. Robert hadn't used any protection. Nor did the thought of protecting herself ever entered her mind.

Dear God, she groaned inwardly, feeling sick inside. *What have I done*? Suddenly, she didn't care if it was any of her business. She had to ask, had to know, even if the number was staggering. "Are there many women in your life?"

Robert instinctively knew why she had asked the question, and felt she had every right to know the truth, whether she believed it or not.

"If you're asking me if I sleep around, the answer is no. You're well aware that I was married, but when she died, I vowed never to become that deeply involved again. That doesn't mean I'm *odd*. It was simply a choice I made and, up until tonight, I've stuck with it."

Maddie made a face. "So what happened tonight that made you break your vow?"

For the first time in his life, Robert didn't analyze a situation to death before giving an explanation. "The truth? Everything. The storm, which seemed to exaggerate my feelings of loneliness, and then you in my robe with nothing on underneath, all curled up on the couch, looking like a little lost kitten, all soft and eager to be held...to be comforted. And suddenly, I wanted to be held, and in my own way, comforted, too. One thing led to another, and here we are."

He stopped for a moment and blew out a frustrated sigh. "Maddie, I honestly didn't mean for things to get out of control. But what happened has happened, and I take full responsibility. For what it's worth, I'm not sorry it happened. On the other hand, if you're expecting me to make some sort of commitment based–"

"I'm not expecting anything," she cut in. She had understood him perfectly. He had let his guard down and gave in to his carnal needs.

Suddenly, Maddie wanted to end the conversation. "I'm exhausted, Robert," she said icily. "I just want to get some sleep."

He moved her face to his and placed a brotherly kiss on her cheek. "Good night, Maddie," he said, and turned on his side. With his back to her, he took only a few moments to fall into the regular breathing rhythm of sleep.

No matter how hurt she felt, Maddie was determined not to give in to the unshed tears that burned her eyes. Feeling used and unwanted again, she curled up into a ball and silently tended her emotional wounds. She was still raw from being humiliated and rejected by Alex, but at this moment, that torment seemed minute compared to the shame and disgrace she now felt. She had actually given herself to a man she didn't know, and all it had taken was a sultry smile, a glass of brandy, and a kiss. She couldn't believe she could be seduced so easily. She had always thought herself as a person of high morals and standards, and could never understand how things like this just happened, as Robert had stated so bluntly. But it had.

Rationalizing the situation didn't help, either. So she had been left at the altar. She wasn't the first. It had happened to hundreds of brides-to-be before her. Yet, she was convinced that most didn't fall into bed a few hours later with the first handsome man who came along. But Maddie had. And now she was paying the price – big time.

Her tortured mind refused to let her sleep, so she lay there listening to Robert's soft, even breathing. She wished now that he hadn't been so honest with her. It was bad enough she behaved like a common trollop, but to have Robert think she was now expecting him to make a commitment, well...

The saddest part of all was that while Robert was using her to rid himself of his loneliness, he had introduced her to a part of herself she never knew existed. She was

35

capable of feeling passion, real passion that took her to Nirvana for the briefest moment before it climaxed in an explosion of pure rapture. Too bad she had never discovered this ultimate pleasure with Alex. For with him, their lovemaking had merely been a comfortable experience. So, she hadn't missed what she had never known. Happy in her own little world, she was content with her meager share of life's goodies and therefore, she never searched for or expected more.

Then suddenly, her world was turned inside out. Alex was gone, along with her apartment, her job, her money *and* her mother's jewelry. Now her only possession was her beat-up old Chevy that sat marooned on the side of the road, its ultimate fate destined for the junk yard.

Her insides now a quivering mass of anxiety, Maddie inched her way out of bed, taking care not to wake the man beside her who was sleeping like a contented baby. Very slowly, she slipped into the robe, then tiptoed to the French doors and parted the curtains. Happy to discover the storm had ended, Maddie stared out at the vast ocean, now calm and serene. Noticing a faint light on the horizon, she wondered what time it was. Since the display on the clock on the night stand next to Robert was hidden from her view, she couldn't tell if the light indicated the approaching dawn, or if it was nothing more than the last streaks of lightening fading away in the distance.

Drawing her gaze from the view, she looked over her shoulder at Robert. Snuggled warmly beneath the covers, he looked so peaceful and satisfied that the urge to pick up a pillow and slam him with it was almost overpowering. How dare he sleep peacefully while her conscience and heart waged a battle royal within her? She was torn with guilt and shame. The longer she looked at him, the stronger those emotions became. Maybe *he* looked upon their sexual encounter as nothing more than a physical release, but to her it had meant something ... *he* had meant something, crazy as it seemed. For how was it possible to feel such a powerful pull of emotion for a complete stranger? Unless...at that moment *her* physical and emotional needs needed tending to, also. And maybe, just maybe, she had thrown caution to the wind and used him to satisfy *her* sudden rush of lust.

The instant that thought crossed her brain, Maddie creased her brow. *What lust?* she asked herself, convinced she was losing her mind. She had never felt lust in her life, not even for Alex. True, she had wanted him enough to marry him, but lust after him? Never.

Too bad, whispered a tiny voice inside her. *Too bad. Especially now that you've discovered just how wonderful sex can be with the right person.*

But apparently Robert doesn't want to be the right person! she almost shouted aloud. That reality sent a rush of adrenalin through her, and she shook her head to clear her mind. She would deal with these facts later. Right now, she had to get away from Robert and take her chances on reaching Alex, even if it meant ... *taking Robert's truck*!

That was it! Why hadn't she thought of that before? She would drive his pickup into Provincetown and head for the police station. There, she would explain her dilemma to the desk sergeant, and ask to be escorted to Alex's apartment. After what Robert had said, Maddie agreed that if she went there alone and unprotected, she would be leaving herself wide open to the possibility of being assaulted, perhaps even killed. She wasn't fool enough to believe that Alex wasn't capable of murder. After all, he had stolen a large sum of money along with her mother's jewelry, and though it pained her to believe he would hurt her before giving them up, she forced herself to be realistic. He very well could.

Too angered now to consider the consequences of her truck-napping, should Robert wake and discover it missing, Maddie dropped to her knees and crawled to where Robert's jeans lay crumpled in a tangled heap at the foot of the bed. Taking care to be especially quiet, she searched through the pockets. When her fingers circled around his key ring, she removed it quickly. Staying on her knees, she made her way to the door, slipped out of the room, and literally flew down the stairs, elated at the thought of getting her money back.

Like a thief in the night, she tiptoed across the semi-darkened living room to the mud room where she removed her clothes from the dryer. Seconds later, she was in front of the fireplace. Behind her she heard a rhythmic clicking noise and turned, realizing it was the dog's claws tapping against the hardwood floor as he approached. The smoldering embers cast just enough light for her to see the dog, who apparently had left his spot in front of the fire sometime during her interlude with Robert, and now stood a short distance away, watching her like a hawk. Whisking on her jacket, she grabbed her scarf and was about to open the front door when she heard Caesar give a low, dangerous growl.

Terror gripped her for a moment, but she willed it away. She couldn't afford to panic now, not with her goal so close. Not only that, she knew she had to move with lightening speed. The dog would be on her any second, keeping her prisoner. Darting for the door, she threw it open and started out, but her escape was thwarted by the animal who lunged and seized her by the heel of her boot.

"Let go!" she hissed, trying to keep her voice low. She really wanted to scream, but common sense told her that one word and Robert would be down in a flash. "N-Nice doggie," she stammered nervously, trying to calm the animal and herself as well. "Let go of my boot and I'll give you something soft and silky to play with." She took the scarf from her pocket and sailed it at the beast. "Here ya go," she said in a sing-song fashion, hoping against hope that he would grab it.

But Caesar ignored it and clamped his teeth firmly into the soft brown leather of her boot. Desperate to be free, Maddie thrust her boot into the animal's throat, but the dog hung on, growling louder with each move she made.

"Sssshhh! You stupid dog!"

"What the hell is going on down there?"

"I hope you're satisfied, you snitch!" she snarled at the animal. Pivoting around on one foot, Maddie grabbed the doorjamb for support.

"Going somewhere?" Robert asked, coming towards her.

Guilt heated her cheeks. She didn't want to tell him she was about to take his truck. What if he refused to let her have it? There wasn't time for an explanation. She had to go. *Now.* "I – uh – I was just going to see about my car."

Robert ignored her flimsy excuse and instructed the dog to release her. When he came to her side, he looked out at the truck in the driveway, then glanced at her. She noticed he was hiding something behind his back. Unable to think her way out of trouble this time, she just stared at the truck, feeling miserable.

"How do you propose to do it?" Robert asked, leaning against the door jam.

Maggie looked at him puzzled. "Do what?"

His lips twisted in amusement. "Unlock your car. Or do you intend to pick it?"

"Don't be ridiculous!" she snapped. "I'll use my–" Her words were cut off by the realization that she had forgotten her purse, which contained her own set of keys.

"They're in here," he said, swinging out her leather bag from behind him.

"Don't tell me. Killer here fetched it for you, right?" she said sarcastically.

Robert grinned. "As the song goes, that's what friends are for."

Furious, she grabbed for the purse, but Robert caught her wrist in mid air. "I'll take these," he said, removing his keys from her clenched fist.

Maddie's heartbeat increased its already rapid pace. "I wasn't going to steal the truck, only borrow it."

He snorted at the confession. "Sure you were."

"It's the truth," she protested. "Think what you want. I have to get to Alex. If I don't leave now, I'll miss him for sure."

Surprisingly, Maddie saw a brief look of hurt cross his face. "How the hell can you still go to him after what we just shared?"

Maddie stiffened her spine, held her head regally, and lied through her teeth. "As far as I'm concerned, *we* didn't share anything but a romp between the sheets. Do yourself a favor and pretend it never happened." She needed to cut him to the quick, to hurt him intensely the way he had hurt her with his comment.

Robert was livid. Feisty was one thing, but lying was something else. He wasn't about to pretend anything. "Oh, it happened, all right," he hissed. "And if I took you in my arms and carried you back to my bed, it would happen again."

"Don't flatter yourself!" she spat out, yet she knew he was right. Deep down she didn't want to leave him, but she couldn't abandon her mission, not when she was so close. "Please, Robert," she pleaded. "Time is running out. Let me take the truck. I promise to return it as soon as I can."

He was silent for a moment, and Maddie held her breath. Was he going to offer to go with her to protect her? Or at the very least, advise her to go to the police department and have Alex arrested for skipping off with her money? By the look on his face, she could tell neither of those thoughts had crossed his mind.

"Here," he said blandly, thrusting the keys into her hand. "Take the truck. But you'll wish you hadn't. This guy is not going to hand anything over to you. He doesn't have to. You have no proof that it's your money or your mother's jewelry. Can't you get that through your thick head? You're running on a fool's errand that could cost you your life. But I guess you have to learn the hard way. So, go ahead," he urged. "Go get him. Just make sure I get my truck back."

* * * * *

An hour and a half later, Maddie was back. "Here," she said, slapping the keys into Robert's palm as soon as he opened the door. "We were too late."

"Who's *we*?"

"Me and the police," she grumbled. "We missed him by an hour."

Robert closed the door behind her. "Who told you?"

She leaned against the wall, drained. "Some friend of his who's leasing his apartment."

Although exhausted and disappointed, she was relieved the ordeal was finally over. There would be no more plotting and scheming to reach him. He was gone and out of her life forever. It was a bitter pill to swallow, but Maddie had no choice now but to accept it.

Robert moved closer and reached out to take her jacket.

"Don't bother," she protested, pulling back. "I'm not staying. I found a gas station open in the center of town. The mechanic agreed to look at my car. He should be along in a couple of minutes with a tow truck. Thanks for lending me your truck."

Robert's voice cracked with sadness when he whispered, "I'm sorry it didn't work out in your favor."

Maddie wasn't moved by his concern. "Really? I would think you'd be gloating over the matter. I even expected an 'I told you so.' Look at you, all bright-eyed and bushy tailed. I would be too if I'd nodded off as soon as–"

"Forgive me for doing that," he apologized. "I feel like a total ass. The only explanation I can give is that when we finished making love, and believe me, I didn't want it to end, I felt so warm and contented, I just fell asleep. Besides, *you* said you were exhausted and wanted to turn in. The next thing I knew, Caesar was barking. I knew you were leaving me and–"

"Forget it." She was so exhausted, her voice had no emotion. "What's done is done."

42

But Robert didn't want to forget it. He wanted to make it up to her. The problem was, he didn't know how. Nervously, he ran his fingers repeatedly through his hair. "Come into the living room and relax over some coffee. I'll meet the mechanic at your car. I'm sure we'll come to some agreement as to what's to be done."

"What's to agree about?" she asked, stifling the urge to yawn. "The tire will be fixed and I'll be on my way."

"I warned you, it might not be that simple," he argued, leading her into the living room. "It's an old car, and it took quite a jolt. Now, stop arguing with me and give me your license, registration, and the name of your insurance company."

Exasperated, Maddie slumped down onto the couch. After rummaging through her purse, she located two of the cards. "Here is my license and my proof of insurance card. The registration is in the glove compartment. Oh, yes, my keys." She tossed them to Robert, who put them into one of his jeans pockets.

On the way to the hall closet, he went into the kitchen, poured her some coffee then set it on the table beside her. Then, giving a nod to Caesar, the two left her to enjoy her coffee in peace.

Maddie took full advantage of the solitude. After hanging her jacket in the hall closet, she pulled off her boots, then reached for the steaming black coffee. Within minutes, the combination of the fire and the coffee reacted like a sedative. Giving in to her exhaustion, she drifted off into a deep sleep.

CHAPTER FOUR

"**W**ho you drag in this time?" muttered a voice tinged with an oriental accent and a hint of sarcasm.

For a minute, Maddie thought she was dreaming. But when she opened her eyes, she saw a tiny, dark, middle-aged woman dressed in a bathrobe and slippers, hovering over her. Wiping her eyes with the back of her hand, Maddie squinted up at the woman. "Who are you?"

"That's Mrs. O'Malley," Robert called out as he entered the room.

At the sound of Robert's voice, the woman padded away from the girl and cornered Robert in the foyer. "Another actress friend?" she snarled, annoyed. "How long *this* one stay?"

"As long as she wants to, my friend," he answered, hanging his coat in the closet. "Now be a good hostess and fix a fresh pot of coffee."

Maddie could hear the woman sputter and groan as she marched off into the kitchen.

Frowning, Robert came to sit beside Maddie. She drew her legs up under herself to allow him enough room to stretch out comfortably.

"Well?" she asked, fixing her gaze on him.

"It's not good news," he said, avoiding her eyes.

"The car *did* have to be towed. Not only did the tie rod snap, but the frame is damaged beyond repair."

"I was afraid of that." She sighed. "How much would it cost if it *can* be repaired?"

Robert gave a cat-like stretch then turned to her and gently clasped her hands in his. "The book value is only a little over six hundred dollars. But the estimate came to a thousand, and Ben gave me a break on that figure when I told him you were a friend of mine. To be honest with you, I'd junk it and get another car. I wouldn't put that kind of money into trying to fix it."

"*A thousand dollars?* Even if the insurance company paid me the six hundred, I don't have the extra four. What am I going to do now? I only have forty-five dollars to my name. How am I supposed to get back to Boston, find another job, and get an apartment on forty-five dollars?"

"Relax," he coaxed, looking beyond her to Mrs. O'Malley who was coming towards them.

Her hands expertly balanced a wooden tray equipped with a stoneware coffee pot, two mugs, and a plate of assorted cookies. When she set the tray down on the coffee table, she gave Maddie an icy stare. "This okay for lady?"

"That'll be fine. Thank you, Mrs. O'Malley," Maddie answered coldly. Even if she preferred something different, she didn't feel at ease to express it.

The housekeeper quickly left them and returned to the kitchen.

Confused, Maddie turned to Robert. "Robert, that woman is obviously Chinese. How come her name is O'Malley?"

He tossed his head back and laughed. "O'Malley is her married name. I met Mei-Lin when I was in China, working with the International Arts Exchange Program. I co-wrote a play with Chinese playwright, Huang Lo Ping, that was supposed to be performed first in Bejing and then on Broadway.

"We had cast Mei-Lin in a small part as a madam. Frank O'Malley was also a cast member. It was love at first sight for both of them. They were married after a short courtship, before the play ended in Bejing. She gave up her career in China to stay in the US with Frank. Unfortunately, Frank had been suffering for years with a heart disorder. He died the night the play opened here in the States."

Maddie frowned at the bad news.

"Mei-Lin couldn't go back to China, and she really couldn't pick up acting here in the United States. Although I had no reason to feel responsible for her, I did, so I offered her the job as my live-in housekeeper. That was three years ago." He paused to take a sip of coffee. "She's a little strange, but she grows on you."

Maddie couldn't resist the urge to ask, "What do you mean, *strange?*"

Robert gave a small sigh. "Mrs. O'Malley has her own routine. She cleans when the mood strikes her, which isn't as often as I'd like. But when she gets going, she's like a blur, and God help you if you get in her way. And every afternoon at two o'clock, she takes to her room where she's got a bottle of Old Grandad and some Tiparillos stashed away in her closet, and she watches her two favorite soap operas. She's a fanatic about them, and nothing short of a major disaster will drag her away from them, especially *Love is for Always*. The main character is a handsome actor who's captured her fancy. Need I say more?"

"Please don't." Maddie giggled, raising her mug to

her lips. They had been so engrossed in the housekeeper's daily routine that she had failed to notice Robert was inching his way alarmingly close to her.

Although he was badly in need of a shower and shave, he smelled wonderful – masculine and natural, not smothered in after-shave lotion the way Alex had always been. Maddie found it very disturbing in a sexual way, and she turned her face from his so he could not detect the effect he was having on her.

Returning the subject safely back to her problem, Maddie asked anxiously, "What am I going to do now? I have no car, no money, no job and no home. I feel as if the world is crashing down on me."

Robert took the coffee mug from her hand and set it on the table. "I have a solution," he said, casually draping his arm across the back of the couch. "You can stay here with me."

"Not on your life!" she said, without so much as a second thought.

"At least hear me out before you refuse," he replied, annoyed. "Do you know how to operate a computer?"

She frowned suspiciously "Of course. Why do you ask?"

"I need a secretary, someone to–"

"Secretary?" Her eyes widened in confusion.

"To type the play I'm working on," he reminded, amazed that she seemed to have forgotten who he was. "That statuette on the bookcase … the one you thought was a bowling trophy? It's called a Tony Award. I won it for one of my plays. Remember?"

She tapped her forehead. "That's right! You did tell me you wrote plays." When she saw the bland scowl on his face, she realized how that sounded. Glancing aside, she mumbled, "Sorry, Robert. I completely forgot you'd told me. Guess I drew a blank for a second there."

"Well, how *could* you remember, as obsessed as you've been to get to your precious *Alex*."

Her mouth dropped open at that scathing comment. He paused with a ragged breath, knowing he had no right to berate her. But like a needle caught in a record's groove, his mind relived their passionate night together, over and over. He could still feel the way her soft, naked body had molded to his, moving against him in a lazy roll that drove him out of his mind. And yet, she still wanted *Alex*.

"Robert ... Robert?" she coaxed.

Her voice brought him out of his self-torturing musings. "Yes. The Tony. I just might be in the running again if I can get this play on paper. The problem is–"

"What do you mean *if* you can get it on paper?" she interrupted. "How have you managed to write your other plays?"

He rolled his eyes and glanced momentarily at the ceiling. "Give me a vintage Royal typewriter any day. That's what I have used for years – a secondhand model I bought when I first started writing. Sadly, it gave up the ghost, and I thought this would be a good time to migrate to the electronic age. I bought a computer recently, but can't seem to get the hang of it. Now I realize I am ill-prepared for that process and really do need help. I considered getting a portable typewriter, but it just doesn't feel the same. I've resorted to writing on legal pads temporarily, but the play needs to be typed, and I can't be bothered learning how to use a computer at this late stage of the game. So you'd be doing me a favor by staying on and typing for me."

As soon as he said it, she stiffened and narrowed her eyes. "Something tells me this *favor* has a string attached."

"If you're implying the job includes being my live-in-lover, I admit I'm highly flattered, but you're greatly mistaken." That was the lie to end all lies. Robert ached to have her in his arms, in his bed, again. And, somehow he knew she knew it. To disguise his fabrication, he hardened his features, withdrew his arm from the back of the couch, and got to his feet.

She looked up at him, mesmerized by his stormy dark eyes staring deeply into hers.

"For your information, *Miss* Price," he snipped, "I never mix business with pleasure. I was merely offering you a job and a place to stay, rent-free, so you could accumulate enough money to get back on your feet."

A blush heated her cheeks and her mouth gaped open. "You would do that for me? Why?"

"Weren't you listening when I explained how Mrs. O'Malley became my housekeeper?" He didn't wait for an answer. "It's called *paying forward* – or *paying back* … whichever term you think fits the situation best. Because there was a time when I was down on my luck too. But I had the good fortune to meet a famous playwright who took me under his wing. He put a roof over my head, taught me the ropes about play-writing, and even produced my first play. When I became successful, I naturally made an effort to repay him, but he wouldn't have any of it. All he did was make me promise to pay it forward. I've done my best to help out others in time of need."

He winced as he recalled Mrs. O'Malley wondering aloud if Maddie was another one of his *actress* friends, and how long *this* one would be staying. Quickly he added,

"Recently I've helped out a few other people in the theater who've suffered a spell of bad luck, and have been rewarded seeing them recover. I am happy to do the same for you – in a similar *platonic* fashion."

"I see," she said, feeling a strange pang of disappointment. "So, your generosity has nothing to do with me personally. You're just carrying out a promise made long ago."

Her brusque comment riled him. Bending down, he grabbed her by the upper arms and pulled her to her feet. A breath apart, he gazed into her liquid blue eyes, and she shook with obvious alarm.

"Forget about what I just told you," he demanded, his voice laced heavily with bitterness. "I need an assistant to help me finish this play. You need a job. I'm offering you one, and I'm willing to pay you handsomely for your work. Unfortunately, it's not a nine-to-five job. Inspiration knows nothing about time clocks. That's why I suggested you live in. Sometimes I begin my work as early as five in the morning, and if it's going well, I often work well past midnight. So, what will it be? Yes or no?"

His offer seemed too good to be true, and Maddie was tempted to blurt out a grateful *yes* before he had a chance to change his mind. But she didn't want to appear too eager, so she hesitated a moment by asking questions. "Computers can be quite confusing. What kind did you get? A Mac or a PC? Is it a laptop or desktop, and did it come with the right software? Because if–"

"I don't know what kind it is," he answered gruffly. "I saw it advertised on one of those home-shopping shows, and the host said a child could operate it. All I know is, it's new, it's expensive, and I'm confident you can handle it."

He released his grip on her arms and ended, "In fact, I'll bet my last dollar you can do anything you put your mind to."

"Anything?" she drawled, leaving him to interpret the double entendre any way he wished.

"Anything," he returned, his lips forming a half-grin. He knew what she was implying and couldn't resist putting it to her point-blank. "No matter how much we may enjoy each other's company in the bedroom, I don't feel comfortable making advances toward you that could be misinterpreted as a quid pro quo mix of business with pleasure. So, let me make one thing perfectly clear. I will never initiate a sexual interlude with you again. It won't be easy. You're just too lovely to resist. The next time we make love – and I have no doubt we will, Maddie – it will have to be initiated by you."

He stood planted before her, smiling that wonderful smile of his. "I hope I won't have to wait too long." With that, he turned away and headed for the front door. "I'm going to clear up this mess with your car. When I get back, I'll take your luggage up to your room. It's the one to the left of mine. Feel free to make yourself comfortable while I'm gone."

* * * * *

As soon as he was out the door, Maddie rushed upstairs and entered her room. To her surprise, she found Mrs. O'Malley bustling about, her arms filled with freshly laundered sheets. The woman kept her back to Maddie as she went about her work. "I done soon, Missy," the housekeeper snapped, sighing heavily as she dropped the linens on the queen-size brass bed.

51

"Oh, please, Mrs. O'Malley," Maddie insisted. "I can do that."

"Good," the older woman replied, obviously relieved to be rid of her duty. "Roads clear now, I go to market. When I come back, I watch my shows."

"Yes," Maddie said, "Mr. Kendall told me a bit about your – uh – routine."

"You no bother me when I watch my shows. You need something, you get it yourself." She turned and waived a scrawny finger at Maddie. "And no make mess. One sloppy person in house enough." She walked to the door and paused with her hand on the doorknob as though trying to remember another rule. "Oh," she said finally. "You and Missah. Kendall share bathroom. Door over there join his room with door on other side. I make beds at nine. I no catch you in his bed, or him in yours. No monkey business. You got it?"

"I got it," Maddie replied gruffly. Imagine the nerve of that woman, implying that she and Robert would be playing musical beds. Apparently Robert hadn't yet informed his housekeeper that she, too, was an employee in the house and not his sleep-in guest.

Had Mrs. O'Malley given her the chance to set the record straight, Maddie would have. But the woman made a speedy exit, leaving Maddie to stare blankly at the door, wondering just exactly what she had gotten herself into.

* * * * *

Maddie was folding the coverlet on the foot of the bed when Robert gave a light tap on her door. He entered without being invited in. "I'll leave these here," he said, setting the suitcases down beside the triple length bureau. He then pointed to the door on the opposite wall. "That's the bathroom," he declared offhandedly. "I'm afraid–"

"I know all about it," Maddie said, cutting him off mid-sentence. "Mrs. O'Malley has already informed me that we share it. She also made it clear that we're not to bed-hop. Really, Robert," she said resentfully, "who's the master of this house? You or her?"

Robert placed a placating hand on her shoulder. "Don't let it bother you. She likes to throw her weight around. It makes her feel needed, I guess. But she's harmless, really."

"Harmless, my foot," she mumbled under her breath. "I'll bet she's got a black belt in karate."

Robert laughed as he stepped over to the chest-of-drawers and opened the bottom drawer. Withdrawing a fluffy white towel, he tossed it to her. "Why don't you take a nice warm shower, then stretch out on the bed for a nap? You didn't sleep all night, and I know you're exhausted. I'll check in on you in a couple of hours, and if you'd like, we can take a stroll on the beach."

Without giving her a chance to respond favorably or not, he turned away and quietly closed the door behind him.

CHAPTER FIVE

*M*addie stood there clutching the bath towel against her breast, feeling as if she were a character in some incredible never-ending dream. She could hardly believe the events that had taken place in such a short span of time, and she had a mega headache pounded in her temples. Dragging her weary body into the bathroom, she hoped to find relief in a nice warm shower.

Ordinarily, she would have appreciated the bath's pastel color coordination and elegant décor, but not today. She stripped off her clothes and turned on the faucets. She stood perfectly still and let the steamy water rain over her aching body until finally, little by little, she could feel her muscles become less tense ... her anger slowly dissipate ... and her frustrations begin to melt away. When she was through, she stepped out onto the soft yellow bath mat. Confident she wouldn't be disturbed, she wrapped the bath towel loosely around herself and padded to the bed, falling asleep as soon as her head hit the pillow.

She slept a dreamless sleep, much to her surprise, and when she woke her headache was gone. She felt refreshed and energized.

Tugging the towel tighter around herself, she opened one of her suitcases and withdrew a pair of pink shorts and matching halter. The temperature in the room had risen a good twenty degrees since she'd fallen asleep, so most likely the weather outside had also warmed considerably. Feeling the need for fresh air, she dropped the outfit onto the bed and went to the French doors. She released the latch and flung the doors open.

Her room opened to a veranda, as did Robert's. Without giving a thought to her skimpy attire, she stepped out onto the redwood porch and scanned the stretch of beach with its pearly sands and rolling waves that slapped against the shore.

"Lovely, isn't it?" The familiar voice caught her by surprise. Embarrassed to have been caught covered only in a towel, she pulled it tighter around herself and started to return to her room.

"Don't go," he said, his voice soft as a caress. She glanced to her right and saw Robert stretched out on a chaise, clad only in a pair of cut-off jeans. A paperback book lay open on his lap. In his hand was a half-empty bottle of beer.

"Really, Robert," she said, blushing at his name sounding like a prayer on her lips, reverent and softly spoken. "I'm not dressed. Let me–"

"You look mighty fine to me," he interrupted, his hot gaze wandering over her with undisguised appreciation. "Here," he said, and he pulled another chaise close beside his. "Come sit by me."

His eyes seemed able to penetrate through the towel, causing her to heat from head to toe. Normally, she would have ignored his invitation and retreated to her room to dress in something more appropriate, but she suddenly liked the way he was looking at her, and she took full advantage of the lustful glint in his eyes by seating herself down very slowly beside him. She ignored the way the soft, warm breeze kept sliding the towel away from her thighs, leaving them fully exposed to Robert's view. Alex had never looked at her that way.

"I trust you had a good nap," he said with great difficulty, his dark eyes mesmerized by her long, shapely legs that had been wound around him just hours before.

"It was more like a coma."

"You needed the rest badly. You've been through quite an ordeal."

She shifted her body ever so slightly towards him, revealing more of the rounded swell of her breasts than she'd wanted to. Making a futile attempt to cover herself, she tried to divert his attention by asking, "What happened to my car?"

Robert reached into the pocket of his cut-offs and pulled out two one hundred dollar bills. Folding the money into a perfect square, he leaned over and gently slid the bills into her cleavage. "The mechanic took it off your hands for what it was worth. It's not much, but you're now two hundred dollars richer than you were when you got here. Now, would you still like to go for that stroll? I managed to persuade Mrs. O'Malley to pack us a gourmet lunch."

"I'll bet it was more like a bribe," she quipped, picturing Robert slipping the woman a cash bonus just to prepare a picnic lunch. Since she hadn't had anything substantial to eat since the day before, the thought of a mouth-watering feast topped off by a stroll along the beach appealed immensely to her. She flashed a wide smile. "Sure, I'd love it."

"Good!" Robert got to his feet. "I'll meet you on the

beach in fifteen minutes."

* * * * *

Maddie was there first. Dressed in her pink shorts and halter that flattered her slim figure to perfection, she wore her hair down and loose, allowing the warm ocean breeze to toss it about her shoulders and back. For the first time in a long time, she felt light-hearted and free.

Still clad in his cut-offs, Robert came towards her laden down with an overflowing picnic basket, an old army blanket, and two towels.

"What's all that for?" she asked, trudging along beside him.

"I used to be a boy scout," he answered proudly. "And if memory serves me right, their motto is 'always be prepared.'"

"Prepared for what?" she asked as they spread the blanket smoothly on the sand.

"You'll see," he teased, dropping down on the blanket. Suddenly, he dug his foot slightly in the sand then brought it up quickly, sending the smooth, warm crystals flying all over her.

"You scoundrel!" she squealed, taking off after him the second he began running along the shore. He made certain not to run so fast that she couldn't catch him. When she did catch up to him, she plunged both hands into the salt water and splashed repeatedly until he was soaked to the skin.

Laughing like children, the two romped and splashed along the water's edge until Maddie pleaded exhaustion. When they reached the blanket, Robert sank to his knees, brushed away the mound of sand that had settled on the blanket, then turned over and stretched out comfortably beside her. The mixture of water and sand had formed lumps of mud along his legs, thighs, and shorts. Automatically, Maddie grabbed a towel and began drying him off.

The feel of his taut muscles beneath her hands made them tremble, and her cheeks flamed. Although he lay there unmoving, Maddie knew he was staring at her – waiting to see just how far she would go before removing the towel. She snatched it away the moment it touched the jagged edges of his shorts.

Robert pulled a face. "Don't stop now. There's still mud on my shorts and chest."

She dropped the towel next to him. "Then you'll have to finish the job yourself."

"Chicken," he teased, picking up the towel.

"Who are you calling a chicken?" she demanded, raising herself up on her knees.

Robert roared with laughter. "You, scaredy cat. Who else?"

"Give me that towel! Nobody calls *me* a chicken!"

He tossed it to her, then sat up straight. Maddie spread the towel across both her hands, then quickly began to rub away the clumps of mud, first from his back, then from his shoulders. When her hands moved down to wipe his furred chest, they slowed down, and unwillingly her heart began pounding so heavily, he could see it fluttering through the thin material of her halter.

"Maddie," he groaned.

"Robert ... no."

"Come here," he murmured, grabbing her by the wrists and pulling her a breath away from him. "I know you

58

want me, so don't deny it. I sense it. I feel it. And you know how much I want you, too. But I promised you I wouldn't make the first move." He grabbed her wrists tighter. "Make it, Maddie. Make it."

For the sake of her sanity, she should have pulled herself free and run from him as fast as possible. But she couldn't move. He was right. She wanted him desperately. Every cell in her body vibrated for his touch ... ached to feel his naked flesh pressed hard against hers ... yearned to once more experience the ecstasy he had brought her to the night before.

In the end, her need for him took possession, and she lowered her face down to his and slowly parted her lips.

Unfortunately, the moment their mouths made contact, something snapped inside Maddie, and she jerked her head back.

"Now, what's wrong?" Robert asked in a daze.

Tears brimmed her eyes, and she slumped back down on the blanket. "Everything, Robert," she half-sobbed. "*Everything.* Right now I feel as if I'm on a roller coaster speeding out of control. One minute I'm fine, and the next I'm flooded with emotions I can't seem to get a grip on. I'm angry and confused. Angry at Alex for not only conning me, but breaking my heart and making me look like a fool, waiting for him at the altar, totally oblivious to the fact that he never intended to marry me at all. And most of all, I'm furious at myself for allowing it to happen. Deep down I always had the gnawing feeling that he never really wanted me ... never really loved me. He probably stuck around because I was the only woman on the planet who refused to see through him. Guess I learned the hard way that money talks, and BS walks, because the minute he got his hands on mine, he left skid marks."

She stopped talking just long enough to wipe her eyes and take a deep breath. "And I'm confused because here I am, one day later, wanting you as if Alex never existed. I don't understand how I can suddenly feel no pain ... no loss...

"Then, last night in your arms, I knew I really didn't love him, either. I couldn't possibly, then turn around and make love to you. Yet, I had to make one last ditch effort to get my money and my mom's jewelry back. So, I took off on your so-called fool's errand. What I didn't realize at the time was that I wasn't running back *to* Alex. I was running away *from* you. I couldn't deal with the fact that you had used me the same way he did ... for your own purpose. The only difference was that you were straight with me. What we engaged in *was* nothing more than a sexual act – two lonely people needing comfort and consolation. When it was over, you made certain that I understood it would never mean anything more."

Robert listened to her, dumbfounded. She had completely misread him. "Maddie, I didn't mean–"

"I was devastated," she admitted, not bothering to let him make some lame excuse for his behavior. "Utterly devastated. Not because you were being truthful, but because you made me feel worthless. So now you want me again. And I'll admit it, I want you, too. But I can't give myself to you just because ... because..." Her emotions were in such a turmoil, she couldn't go on.

Robert closed his eyes for a moment and digested her confession, remembering the night he had unburdened himself to Andy. He never forgot his friend's words of wisdom. Now it was his turn to enlighten Maddie ... that is, if she'd stay put long enough to listen. Tenderly, he reached out for her hands and grasped them firmly.

"For what it's worth, Maddie, you're not the only one who's loved and lost, or has been taken advantage of. Given enough time, it happens to all of us. The difference is that some of us choose to hold on to the pain instead of putting it behind us and getting on with our lives. Like fools, we deal with it by either avoiding entanglements altogether, or we build a comfort wall around ourselves. We act indifferent, aloof, and uncaring. But it's only a façade, a means of self-preservation. Trust me. I'm an expert at building walls. I've been hiding for a very long time behind the ones that I've built." He paused a moment and shook his head in retrospect. "What a waste."

Maddie didn't want to hear any more. "Are you through?"

She sounded so damn smug, Robert pulled her back into his arms. "No, I'm not through. I was making a point. Listen, and you just might learn something.

"Since my wife died, there have been several women who've come into my life. Decent women, worthy of being loved. But I refused to let them inside my heart and my bed because I didn't want to take the chance of getting hurt again. That's why I told you not to assume that because we'd made love, you shouldn't be expecting me to make a commitment. At the time, I was protecting myself. However, I know I *never* told you it could never mean anything more. The truth is, honey, it means more to me than I can admit. And now, every time I look into your beautiful face, or come anywhere near you, I feel that wall crumbling brick by brick. *Brick by brick*," he repeated as he lowered her down and moved his mouth softly over hers.

61

Like the night before, Maddie became putty in his hands, rolling above then below him as their mouths fused together and their tongues explored each other's in a searing kiss.

Mindless with wanting him, Maddie arched her back slightly enough to allow Robert to unsnap her halter. In breathless anticipation, she waited while he pushed the top away and brought his hand back to brush lightly across her button-hard nipple. She felt no shame, no modesty, only a driving need for the touch of his lips on her breast. Rockets spiraling in her head, she fumbled with the snap on his shorts, pulling at them hard and swift as the zipper gave away. She then slid her hands along the curves of his buttocks and wiggled the shorts down until he could kick them away with his feet.

In slow motion, he rolled her on top of him, raining sweet kisses across her breasts and down the soft swell of her stomach. "Good God, Maddie," he groaned, taking her hand and pressing it against his hardness. "You're driving me crazy."

"Good," she breathed, relishing the knowledge that she was able to arouse him to this pitch. When he drew her nipple into his mouth, she pushed his hand to the elastic band on her shorts. Leveling herself no more than an inch, she held her body rigid while Robert slid the shorts over her hips, gliding them down along her legs with his knees.

A soft, gentle breeze cooled their passion just long enough for Robert to reach out and grab one end of the blanket. Then tossing it over them, they rolled over and over until they were wrapped together in a flannel cocoon. The instant he pressed his palm on her navel, she flowered under his touch, urging his fingers down lower to the sensitive vee between her legs. Fire raced through her inner thighs and she arched against the hand that was driving her mad.

Wanting to bring her to the same level of sweet torture, Robert continued his erotic probing, and Maddie moaned aloud in a rapturous sigh when his fingers made contact with her greatest source of pleasure.

His heartbeat hammered in cadence with hers, and finally groaned, "Maddie, please ... please. I can't stand it anymore!"

Neither could she. The pleasure he would bring her to was only a torturous moment away. Guiding him with her hand, she parted her thighs and with one swift thrust he filled her aching void, both of them savoring every minute of it. He was clutching her so tightly she could scarcely breathe. Not that she cared. Moments later, under the warmth of the bright September sun, with the crashing waves a soothing backdrop to her rapturous sighs, she and Robert rose together in mutual ecstasy. Maddie smiled. Another brick had been chipped away.

* * * * *

Robert was fastening the snap on Maddie's halter when she tilted her head back slightly to face him. For a moment, time hung suspended as the two gazed longingly at one another. Maddie felt she was drowning in the depths of Robert's smoky dark eyes that smoldered seductively in the afterglow of their lovemaking.

"Maddie–" he started, then stopped himself. He wanted to tell her she had a gridlock on his heart, perhaps even on his soul. He wanted her to know that their lovemaking was *not* a carnal act he had taken lightly. Quite the contrary. He wanted to say that he was falling in love with her. But he held back. It was too soon to make such a declaration. He was also afraid she wouldn't believe him. Instead, he suggested, "What do you say we postpone that walk? My legs feel like rubber bands."

"So do mine." She blushed and dragged her eyes away. It was happening, she told herself. He was beginning to fall in love with her. He had almost admitted it. Almost.

"Must be the salt air," he said, a wry grin twisting his mouth as he leaned back on his elbows.

She laughed while tousling his wavy hair with her fingers, then sat up straight. "What do you say we eat? I'm starved."

"Me too." He reached across the blanket and dragged the picnic basket closer. When he flipped back the checkered cloth, he licked his lips. "Ah, bless that crazy housekeeper of mine. She fixed us her special oriental chicken wings, egg rolls, and homemade brownies."

"What? No fortune cookies?" Maddie quipped, digging out the food and paper plates.

Robert took the plastic containers and spread them on the blanket. "Who needs fortune cookies?" he commented, giving her a sly little wink. "I happen to have an invisible crystal ball that lets me see into the future."

Maddie let the remark pass for a minute while she placed an ample portion of the food on their plates. Then curling up in a comfortable position, she looked at him and drawled in a mystical voice, "Then tell me, O Swami, what do you see in your crystal ball?"

Just to amuse her, he decided to play the game to the hilt. Assuming the role of an East Indian guru, he closed his eyes, crossed his legs into a yoga position, and rocked back and forth, pretending to transcend into the spirit world. His face expressionless, he finally began to speak. "Ah, my child," he murmured in a high-pitched monotonous chant, "as my mind's eye gazes into the crystal ball, I see a tall, dark, exceptionally handsome man who is making mad passionate love to you. And he's good, too!"

Maddie let out a giggle. "Do you know the man's name?"

Robert pressed his fingers tightly over his eyes. "His name begins with an 'R' – an 'R' that stands for romance, rapture, and ... and ... writing!"

"Writing?" she squealed, biting on a chicken wing. "Writing doesn't start with an 'R' – unless it does in Swami school." She was laughing so hard, the tears were streaming down her cheeks.

"Silence!" Robert commanded. "You are breaking the Swami's concentration." He let out a long, drawn-out sigh, pretending to be annoyed. "This man, whose name begins with an 'R,'" he repeated, "is now working your fingers to the bone. You're begging for mercy, but he does not hear you. He is making you work for a pittance with no time off, no medical benefits, and no 401K plan."

Playfully, Maddie pursed her lips and placed her hands on her hips. "I don't think I like this man whose name begins with an 'R.'"

"On the contrary," he opposed, "I see you falling madly in love with him."

Brazenly she interrupted him again. "Is he falling in love with *me*?"

Again, Robert wanted to turn to her, take her into his arms and say yes, but he steeled himself and answered sternly, "This is not a quiz. This is a vision. Please, let

Swami continue."

"Oh, go ahead." She laughed, licking her fingers.

"Thank you." He bowed. "Now, where was I? Ah, yes. Swami sees you catering to his every whim, rushing to his side when he snaps his fingers, and giving his faithful dog a bath every Saturday night."

"Gimme a break," she quipped. "You're the kind of sorcerer that gives fortunetellers a bad name. You're a fake." Yet, a flame sparked deep inside as she recalled the part where he'd said she was falling madly in love with him. Why he wouldn't answer her question about his feelings was another matter ... a matter she would deal with later.

* * * * *

As soon as the picnic was over, Robert's playfulness vanished. He turned onto his stomach and adopted a pensive attitude. Bothered by this sudden change in him, Maddie moved closer, turned on her side, and asked what was going through his mind.

He answered immediately. "The play I'm working on has hit a snag. It's possible I might have writer's block, or maybe it's just lack of research."

"Maybe I can help," she offered, watching him closely as he made small circles in the sand.

"Maybe you can. The story centers around a male detective who passes himself off as a woman and takes up residence in a rooming house for aspiring young models. Two of the girls have been murdered, and it's his assignment to solve the case."

Maddie couldn't wait for him to finish. Eyes rounded wide, she exclaimed, "Robert, I don't believe it! I was a receptionist for a private detective agency. I answered the phones, set up appointments, typed their reports, and prepared their files. And because I enjoyed it so much, I became a pretty good sleuth myself. I remember one case where I did some snooping around on my own. The agency didn't have much pertinent information at the time. But, I had a hunch. I told the guys what I thought, and I was right on the money. Because of *me,* they nabbed a man who was poisoning his about-to-be-ex-wife, little by little. Seems she was heavily insured, and he wanted her dead for the cash before the divorce was granted. It had all the markings of a typical Grade B movie plot."

Robert looked at her, stunned. "You really helped nail the guy?"

"Sure I did. Why? Does that surprise you?"

He looked at her thoughtfully, then lowered his gaze to the blanket. Maddie watched intently while he folded and refolded the frayed edges of the material. "I don't mean to sound wishy-washy," he replied, "but it does and it doesn't."

Maddie wrinkled her nose. "What kind of answer is that?"

An unreadable expression crossed Robert's face. "It doesn't surprise me because, as I told you before, I believe you can do anything you set your mind to. On the other hand it does. Because for a woman who just proved to be a pretty good sleuth, you were totally blind when it came to solving your own case. Talk about not seeing the forest for the trees."

Maddie gave him a puzzled look. "What are you talking about?"

"I'm talking about Alex. He was a con artist and you couldn't see it. Or more than likely, you didn't want to see it. I'm sure he promised you the moon when he got on his feet. But times are hard now, and people are losing their jobs every day. What money they do have is being spent on necessities, not paintings. Even if he sold one periodically for a few hundred dollars, there's no way he was able to make enough money to support himself, which means that you must have been supporting him, just as you supported your father."

He paused to open a can of soda. After he took a healthy gulp, he continued. "Sorry to say, but Alex was too street smart for you. You're a giver not a taker, and he milked you for all you were worth. For him, latching on to you was like hitting the lottery. I know it sounds cruel, because you really want to believe he loved you, but once the seed of doubt was planted in your mind, why didn't you dump him? He certainly wasn't going to leave on his own and forfeit all that money. So, he proposed. But once he knew where the money was, he didn't need to go through with the wedding. Now the guy is history. Believe me, you're better off finding out the truth about him now rather than later."

Maddie's face twisted in a scowl. "Are you through preaching now?"

"No, I'm not. I just want to add that you're a beautiful woman, inside and out. And if you had listened to your instincts and dumped him first, you would've found someone deserving of you. And today you'd still have your job, your apartment, your money *and* your car."

Maddie raised her eyes heavenward, waiting patiently until he finished. "That's all very true. But, you're forgetting something. I also wouldn't have met *you*."

Robert lay there a few minutes, pondering what

she'd just said. She was right. Had *any* of the events been different, he wouldn't have met her, been captivated by her, made love to her. He was about to voice his thoughts when he glanced at his wristwatch. "Good god!" he exclaimed, noting the time. "We'd better get back to the house. I didn't realize it was so late."

Late for what? Maddie wondered as they rose to their feet and began folding the blanket.

As soon as they entered the house, Robert called out to his housekeeper. His brow creased in perplexity when she didn't answer. Shrugging it off for a moment, he went into the kitchen, set the picnic basket down on the counter, then asked Maddie to put the blanket into the washing machine.

Both now calling out to the older woman, they entered the living room and discovered Mrs. O'Malley sprawled out on the sofa. An afghan was casually thrown over her legs, and a damp wash cloth covered her brow. Robert was relieved to see her until he noticed the half-empty glass of Old Grandad clutched tightly in her hand.

Maddie shot a frightened look his way as they hurried to her side. Fearing she'd had a spell of some sort, Maddie watched Robert sink to his knees beside her while Maddie took the glass and set it on the coffee table. Her keen eye noticed that the liquor bottle on the end table was turned over and empty, and that Caesar was busy licking the remnants that had spilled onto the carpet. It was the first time Maddie's presence had no ill effect on the dog.

"Mei-Lin, open your eyes and look at me." Robert's voice broke with emotion. While he spoke, he pressed her hot, flushed cheeks with the back of his hand.

A loud hiccup erupted from Mrs. O'Malley, and she burst into tears. "My Leon..." she slurred, obviously brokenhearted. "Heart attack ... don't look good ... maybe not make it."

As soon as she disclosed the cause of her grief, Robert's body stiffened. He turned and looked at Maddie, disgust spreading across his face.

"Who's Leon?" Maddie asked nervously, assuming it was probably a relative of the bereaved and quite inebriated woman.

Robert looked back down at his housekeeper with unbelieving eyes and stated blatantly, "Leon is that actor on the soap opera I told you about. My guess is that his contract is about to expire, and his fate now hangs in the balance of the script writers."

Squelching the urge to laugh, Maddie moved away and perched herself on the arm of a nearby chair. It was inconceivable to her that a man who was merely an actor on a television series had such a profound impact on this poor soul. And yet, it was amusing to discover that not only she, but the dog, had taken to the bottle over this fantasy crisis and were now both stoned to the gills.

"What are you going to do about this?" Maddie asked, biting hard on her bottom lip to keep from giggling.

"Not a bloody thing," Robert remarked dryly. "Best she sleeps it off." He rose to his full height and walked into the foyer, waving Maddie on. They stopped before a room at the end of the hall and to the right of the staircase. He unlocked the door with a skeleton key and motioned her to enter.

"This is my office, he said, closing the door behind them. Then he stepped around to the back of a long mahogany desk. Without looking at her, he began describing the contents of the drawers.

"I keep the play I'm working on in the top drawer. There are about fifty pages written in long hand on a yellow legal pad. I'd like you to transcribe them onto the computer. If you need help figuring out the computer, the manual is in the same drawer. The rest of the drawers contain everything else you'll need. The printer is on that rollaway stand behind you. I've never used it. If you need help with it, it also has a manual. I think that's all you'll need for tonight's work. I won't have time to proofread the draft this evening, so just leave it in a folder in the top drawer. I'll get to it in the morning."

Maddie looked at him in disbelief. Suddenly, his whole demeanor had changed. He had spoken to her with an air of indifference as one would an employee, and not the love partner she'd become just a short time ago. He left her standing there looking at his back as he headed for the door. When he grasped the doorknob, he spoke without so much as a glance her way. "The key is on the desk. I want this room locked whenever you're not in here. Caesar loves to chew up my papers, and Mrs. O'Malley is itching to get in here and clean. She loves to tidy up other people's chaos as much as she loves to create her own."

When he closed the door behind him, Maddie leaned against the desk and looked with unseeing eyes around the room. Scrambling through her mind were the instructions he'd laid out for her in precise detail. She'd understood him completely, so there had been no need for questions, at least not ones concerning the job that awaited her. What she didn't understand was his blasé attitude towards her, plus the fact that he wouldn't have time tonight to proofread her work.

I'll get to it in the morning, he had said, dryly. *Why*

not tonight? She asked herself, searching her mind for an answer that wouldn't come.

She was still deep in thought when she heard the sound of Robert's footsteps moving rapidly in his room directly above the office. Imagining he had gone to change his clothes, she decided to do the same. Taking the key from the desk, she locked the door behind her and hurried up the stairs.

The sound of his off-key singing in the shower made her groan. She quickly removed her shorts and halter and donned a pair of old jeans and a white, long sleeve blouse. Feeling blue and dejected, she gave her hair a vigorous brushing. Not caring how she looked, she closed the door to her room and headed back to his office.

Because she had eaten so heartily, she didn't feel hungry. She decided to dig in and get the job done as quickly as possible.

She was seated at the computer, sorting out the handwritten pages, when Robert entered the room. Seething inside, she ignored him. He came and positioned himself directly in front of her. Maddie dropped the papers onto the desk and raised her eyes to him. Instantly, her heart caught in her throat. Dressed in a wine-colored dinner jacket, ruffled shirt and silk slacks, he looked fantastic. Before she had a chance to compliment him, Robert announced in a light, airy voice, "I have a special engagement tonight, Maddie. It was preplanned far in advance, so it's impossible for me to break it. Sorry to leave you with so much work to do alone." His manner of speaking was so cool, so perfunctory, she doubted his sincerity. As far as she was concerned, he had never intended to break his date – work or no work.

Leaning back against her seat, Maddie suffered a stabbing pain in her heart as the intimacy they had shared on the beach came quickly to mind. But she was determined not to show it. "Have a good time," she said tightly, feeling a lump rise in her throat. She then turned in her seat, looked away, and returned to her work.

Despite the agonizing pull in his heart for being so secretive, he reached down and threaded his fingers through the flowing waves that cascaded over her shoulders. "I'll be late," he said, tugging at a silky strand. "Don't wait up for me." He planted a light kiss on the top of her head, turned, and left the room.

CHAPTER SIX

The minute she heard the front door close, Maddie jumped from her seat and hurried to the side window. Eyes flinty with a mixture of anger and jealousy, she pushed aside the thin curtains and watched as Robert maneuvered a silver gray Cadillac around the truck and down the length of the driveway. "How can you do this to me?" she shouted, pounding her fist against the closed window.

A knot twisted painfully in her stomach as she recalled their torrid lovemaking on the beach. They had been so happy, and Robert had acted as if he never wanted to leave her side. Now, some two hours later, he had a special engagement he couldn't break. One that required formal attire. One, she was certain, involved another woman.

Unaware that a teardrop had rolled its way slowly down her cheek, she whisked it away with the flick of her finger when it reached the corner of her mouth. Once the car was out of sight, she left the window and slumped back down on the chair behind the desk. She closed her eyes tightly to press back the tears that threatened to spill, then drew a long, ragged breath and struggled for control. It came when she realized that Robert Kendall was a lying, arrogant bastard who had confessed with such conviction, that he had remained celibate until she came along and changed everything.

What a crock, she told herself, digging her nails into her palms. And *he* had the nerve to call *Alex* a con artist!

What was even more disturbing was that she had fallen for *his* sob story, hook, line and sinker, as well. She hadn't learned a thing from her experience with Alex. Not once, but twice she had given herself to Robert. And like the normal male he claimed to be, he jumped at the opportunity she made so easily available to him. He had craved her touch, her kiss, her body, and had taken her with a hunger like a man starved for love. Then she gave a chuckle remembering the oriental lunch which Robert had consumed with such enthusiasm, and the old adage came to mind: *Eat Chinese food and an hour later you're hungry again.* So Robert was hungry again. But this time it wasn't for her.

Muttering an oath, she flung the papers down. They flew haphazardly over the desk, but Maddie didn't care. All she could think about was the woman who would be taking her place in Robert's arms tonight. No doubt she would not only be breathtakingly beautiful, but certainly eager to give her body to Robert just as Maddie herself had.

A savage desire to do them both bodily harm exceeded her capacity to think rationally, so Maddie gathered up the papers, put them in order, and began taking out her anger on the computer's keyboard. For her, work had always been a panacea to everything. Tonight it would be her salvation. For if she thought about Robert and that woman one more second, she surely would have gone mad.

* * * * *

Two hours later, the ache that had settled in her lower back became so extreme, she was forced to call a halt to her work. What she needed was a breath of fresh air, so she locked the door to the office, went up to her room and out onto the veranda.

This night was made for lovers, she thought, feeling not only disappointed, but lonely and blue. A low, full moon drifted in and out of the clouds while the stars shimmered like diamonds above the velvety black water. The slow rhythm of the lapping waves on the shoreline beckoned her to sample its refreshing coolness. So she slowly walked down the steps, removing her sandals as she went. Walking leisurely towards the shore and the spot where she and Robert had made love, she hugged herself, delighting in the gentle balmy breeze and the play of the moon and the clouds above her.

She was so lost in the beauty of the night that at first she didn't hear the sound of Robert's laughter echoing in the distance. As it became louder and clearer, anxiety gripped her, making her heart hammer rapidly in her chest.

Quickly she scanned the beach, looking for a place to hide. All she could see was the beach house. But the light from the moon blanketed the steps to the veranda, enabling anyone strolling along the beach to spot her presence. So, she scurried off to the left, to a short, grassy sand dune. Slumping down behind it, she prayed Robert and the woman he was with wouldn't discover her hiding place. When their voices became louder with each approaching step, Maddie assumed they were no more than ten or twelve yards away.

And then there was nothing. No talking ... no laughing ... no nothing. The silence drove her crazy. *What were they doing?* she wondered, getting down on all fours.

One part of her didn't want to know. The other had to. Peeking around the grassy dune, she watched with horrified eyes as the two figures melded into one silhouette.

Although she couldn't be sure, she surmised Robert was kissing the woman. The realization tore into her heart like a knife. Choking back a sob, she pounded her fist in the sand like an irascible child. With each vicious pounding, she whispered his name repeatedly in despair, wishing she were somewhere else – anywhere but here. Trapped behind the sand dune, she could do nothing but send up a silent prayer that she would not have to witness a love scene between the two. For at this moment, the sight of their liquid forms merged together, so hypnotic in the moonlight, was just too much to take. Yet, Maddie found it impossible to turn her eyes away.

Mesmerized, she continued to stare at them, straining her neck to observe every move they made. Oddly enough, as Robert bent to coax his date down onto the sand, the most wonderful thing happened. Caesar began galloping along the beach, barking loudly the minute he caught sight of his master's figure etched in the moonlight.

Tears of joy flooded Maddie's eyes. She was never so happy to see that horrible beast in her life. With a hand cupped over her mouth, she stifled an exhilarating laugh, then watched as the three headed back down the beach and away from her hiding place.

As soon as they were out of sight, Maddie dashed for the veranda, snatched her sandals, flew up the steps, and slammed the French doors shut behind her. Completely out of breath, she slumped against the doors, gasping for air.

For what seemed an eternity, she remained there, listening to the pounding of her heart, devastated to think that, had the dog not come along at precisely the right moment, Robert would have made love to the woman. Again, she could feel the torment and fury building to a boiling point, and she knew if she didn't do something about it fast, she'd scream.

She stripped off her clothes and hurled them angrily against the door at the opposite side of the room. When that spontaneous tantrum failed to defuse her fury, she resorted to her customary cold shower. Grabbing two towels from the drawer in the chest, she marched into the bathroom and stepped into the tub. With the snap of her wrist, she turned on the cold tap and raised her head high, gasping audibly when the icy water hit her feverish body. She began to shiver uncontrollably and even found it difficult to breathe. But she needed this shock to her system. It made her see how naïve she had been with both Alex and Robert. She had believed their lies ... trusted them with her heart, and in the end she was left penniless, brokenhearted, and betrayed.

The water was so cold, she couldn't think any longer, so she turned the faucets to warm and leaned back against the cool tiles, sighing deeply as the tepid water poured over her naked body. She closed her eyes and let the soothing sensations overtake her. Then, with a large, soft sponge, she began to direct the water first over her shoulders, then down the narrow crevice between her soft, full breasts.

She shivered again as the touch, in her imaginings, became not her own, but Robert's. Unwillingly she longed for him and the warmth of his hard muscular body pressing into hers as it had that afternoon. When the taunting reverie brought tears rushing to the surface, she willed herself back to reality and rasped aloud, "Get a grip, girl! Open your eyes and see Robert for what he really is! He's a son of a bitch, and I'm the world's biggest fool for allowing myself to get involved with him!"

More angry with herself than with Robert, she turned off the taps and reached around the curtain to the vanity for both towels. She twisted one around her head turban style. Then, wrapping the other around herself, she pushed back the shower curtain. Immediately, she went cold all over. There, leaning against the vanity was Robert, his dark, lean torso naked, with a towel draped loosely around his hips.

Mortified, she stared at him, speechless. He was quick to break the silence. "So, you're a fool for getting involved with me, eh, Maddie?" he mocked, crossing his arms casually across the broad expanse of his chest.

Maddie glared at him. "How dare you come in while I'm showering! Doesn't a person have any privacy around here?"

His lips twisted in a wry smile. "I might ask you the same question."

Maddie pulled the towel higher. "What question?"

"Doesn't a person have any privacy around here?"

Carefully she stepped out of the shower and moved past him, her eyes automatically falling to the curves of his hips. The towel was tied so loosely that one quick move, and it would have fallen to the floor. "I don't know what you're talking about," she replied haughtily, trying to ignore the butterflies in her stomach.

Robert turned and caught her by the shoulders. "I'm talking about my walk on the beach. Did you really believe you were safely hidden by the sand dune?"

Maddie was stunned. "You saw me?"

Robert's eyes danced as he let his gaze traveled over her shocked face, then down to the fullness of her breasts barely concealed by the towel. "Not at first," he admitted, following her out of the bathroom. "But as I got nearer the house, I noticed the French doors to your room were open, and the light was on. With the moonlight shining across the dune, it didn't take much to figure out you were playing detective ... again."

He turned his back and moved slowly over to her bed. "Why were you spying on us, Maddie?"

She never heard his question. She just stared in awe at the semi-nakedness of his body that was now stretched out on her bed as if he had all the right in the world to be there. For a moment, she couldn't think ... couldn't speak. She could only gawk at him and drink in his magnificent form. He was the most virile man she had ever seen, and she continued to gaze at him blankly as if in a trance.

When she finally found her voice, she blurted out the question that had plagued her since she saw Robert and the woman embracing in the moonlight. "Who is she, Robert?"

At first, something held him back, as though he was not yet ready to answer her. Then his expression relaxed. Smiling, he lifted himself up slightly and pulled Maddie down on the bed beside him. "She's just a good friend, Maddie, and nothing more. Seems to me we've covered the subject of women in my life already. But I can see by the look on your face, you don't believe me."

"After what I saw, how can you expect me to believe anything you say?"

"Because I wouldn't lie to you."

Maddie's control snapped. "The hell you wouldn't. You know I saw you. I really didn't expect you to admit that you were having an affair with – with whatever her name is."

Robert's lips tightened in a thin line. "Her name is Andrea, and we're not having an affair. Besides, I could never make love to another woman after you."

Maddie's innermost instincts told her he was lying. But before she had a chance to dispute him, Robert loosened the towel around his hips exposing himself fully to her view. She held her breath when his fingers untied the knot in hers. When it came undone, he reached for her and curled her against him, breathing in her clean, fresh scent. Wildfire raced through her veins, but her anger was stronger, and she used it to fuel the fury that had been locked inside her the entire night. With balled fists she pulled herself upright. "No, Robert! You can't have everything you want. And friend or no friend, if Caesar hadn't come along, you most certainly would have made love to that ... that *Andrea*, and you wouldn't be in my room now." Wrinkling her nose, she tore her gaze away. "Wouldn't you know she'd have a provocative name like *Andrea*?"

Robert steeled himself to keep from smiling. "It is rather provocative, now that you mention it."

An inner ache made its way to Maddie's heart, and she used all her strength to challenge him. "Well, whatever her name is, it's not the issue here. The point is that even though you knew I was watching, you *still* pulled her close and kissed her! Now, try to deny *that!*"

"I will," he murmured. "I didn't kiss her."

"Bull!" she retorted. "I saw you coaxing her down onto the sand. Now tell me you weren't going to perform your Swami act for *her*."

The look in Robert's eyes grew soft. "Did what you *think* you saw really hurt you?"

"Yes, it did," she answered. "I'm not promiscuous

like I suspect you truly are. And, no matter how much you deny it, you have to admit that what you appeared to be doing with *Andrea* couldn't be interpreted as anything but sexual. I … I could never have done what you did on the beach tonight unless I was in love–" She caught herself in mid-sentence, appalled at what she had admitted unintentionally. She bit her lower lip with that slip of the tongue, and abruptly turned her head away.

God, was it true? Was there actually such a thing as love at first sight? And had it happened to her? Two days ago she would have denied it. But then she met Robert, and her whole manner of thinking, of conducting herself, had changed. From the beginning, his very presence had taken control of her, sending sexual desire throughout her body. Even now as they quarreled, deep feelings for him were there. Only this time she refused to permit those feelings to dominate her. Like it or not, the time had come to regain control of her life, to wipe the slate clean and begin a new one. That could only be accomplished by leaving his house. The sooner the better.

The decision made, Maddie pulled away from him. Fastening the towel around herself, she jumped off the bed.

As if Robert could read her mind, he moved swiftly to stop her. Stretching himself full-length across the bed, he caught her by the upper arm and, with one swift move, pulled her back onto the bed beside him. With both hands, he gently turned her face to meet his anguished look. "You're leaving here, aren't you?"

There was something in his voice that made her eye him warily. "Yes. This arrangement isn't working out. You know it, and so do I."

"I don't know any such thing," he said, rubbing his

thumb softly against her cheek. "The only thing I know is that you're in love with me. You admitted it."

"I lied!" she spat viciously, hating herself for lying again.

"No, you didn't."

Her nerves now at the breaking point, she knew if this fight continued for one more minute, she would become completely undone, giving him an even greater advantage over her than he already had. She slid to the end of the bed and, raising her chin in a defiant manner, said, "Please leave, Robert, this discussion is–"

"This whole thing is about my so-called relationship with Andrea, isn't it?" he blurted.

She wanted to say yes, but she wouldn't give him the satisfaction. A lump the size of a baseball formed in her throat. She turned her eyes away and said in a voice just above a whisper, "Your relationship with her is none of my business."

Robert glared at her. "You're lying. I believe she *is* the reason you want to leave. You're jealous of her!"

That did it. Jumping to her feet, Maddie ran to the door and flung it open. Furious, she hissed, "I don't care if this *is* your house. Get out! *Now!*"

Immediately, Robert's eyes took on a hard glint, like cold, tempered steel. Keeping them locked with hers, he quickly fastened the towel around his waist and shot to his feet. When he reached the door, he looked back at her and said, "You're wrong about me, Maddie, dead wrong. No matter what you think you saw on the beach tonight, I wasn't going to make love to her. I told you so. I gave you my word." He turned and closed the door gently behind him.

* * * * *

An eternity passed before Robert's erratic breathing came under control. Pacing in his room, he struggled with the fact that he was about to lose Maddie, all because of a stupid little stunt cooked up by Andy to prove his acting ability beyond any doubt.

Robert stopped in front of the French doors leading to the veranda beyond and shook his head in misery. It had been Andy's idea to walk on the beach and stop below Maddie's window to see if he could convince her he was a woman. Robert instinctively knew it was a bad idea and had balked adamantly against it, calling it an act of cruelty. But Andy insisted, so determined he was to test his acting skills in a real trial 'in the field.' And Robert had given his word not to reveal Andy's secret to anyone, so he couldn't just tell Maddie the truth.

In his defense, Andy was quick to reassure that Maddie, if she was fooled at first, wouldn't remain angry for long – especially after Robert had told him how he and Maddie had made love openly under the warm September sun that afternoon. The fiery redhead had even admitted to feeling jealous – all part of his 'in character' performance, Robert assumed. Of course Robert didn't share any details of how he had gloried in the feel of Maddie's fingertips tracing the contours of his body, or how he had become mindless under the rain of her soft, tender kisses that had left him breathless, or the way she circled her velvety soft thighs around his waist and had urged him deep inside her…

A nervous flutter attacked Robert's stomach, and he ran his fingers through his hair repeatedly at the memory.

No wonder Maddie was devastated by the sight of him on the beach with what she assumed was another woman. Had the tables been turned, he would have believed the same thing – that he'd been heartlessly betrayed.

How could I have been so stupid to let Andy talk me into something like this?

The fluttering in is stomach turned into a sharp pain. He felt like smashing his fist through the wall to destroy the barrier separating him from Maddie. He'd screwed up royally, now the damage was done, and despite what his friend might have been thinking when he talked him into playing along with that stupid stunt, Robert knew in his heart that he had only himself to blame for this mess.

He forced his rapid breathing to calm. Maddie deserved to know the truth about Andy-Andrea, and most of all, about his own feelings for her. But now was not the time to discuss things with her. She was angry and wouldn't listen to or believe a word he told her. And Andy had already gone home, leaving no opportunity to provide evidence showing what he claimed was actually true. He'd have to wait until tomorrow to talk to her, after she'd cooled down. He'd ask Andy to come over again tomorrow morning in full regalia, then have him explain in his own words the reason behind his charade. Once Maddie understood it was all about Andy and his need to prove to himself he could play the part perfectly, she'd have no reason to be angry, no reason to leave. And then ... then he could tell her everything ... the truth about his feelings for her. *Tomorrow night at the party.*

"Yes," he whispered aloud, his plan of action formulating in his mind as if by magic. He'd set the stage for his apology – and his proposal. The right timing, the right music – everything needed to be absolutely perfect to ensure she couldn't possibly refuse him.

Happy to be relieved of the burden that weighed heavily on his heart, he turned from the veranda and set about putting things in motion. "I'll tell her everything while we're dancing to ... *Unforgettable*."

CHAPTER SEVEN

*M*addie was dressed and waiting for Mrs. O'Malley when she rapped softly on her bedroom door at 9:00 a.m. sharp. They greeted each other with their usual warmth. Amazingly Maddie had somehow won over the older woman in the few days she'd been there.

As Mrs. O'Malley walked over to the French doors and opened them wide, allowing the fresh air and bright sunshine to fill the room, Maddie asked her if she could borrow her car for a few hours. The question piqued the housekeeper's curiosity, and she turned to look at Maddie. "Now you go, no breakfast?" She tilted her head and narrowed her gaze. "Dark circles under eyes. You no sleep good last night. Missah Kendall, he no sleep good too." She shrugged. "It something in water?"

Maddie smiled. "Funny you should say that. My father used that term every time someone did something strange. 'Must be something in the water,' he'd say."

After shaking her head in retrospect, she sat down on the edge of the bed and looked solemnly at the housekeeper. "I can't stay here any longer, Mrs. O'Malley. Mr. Kendall and I ... well ... we don't exactly see eye to eye. So I'd like to get a newspaper and see if there are any rooms for rent and also find out what jobs are available."

The housekeeper digested the news for a moment before she spoke. "Car keys in kitchen on breadbox. But you stop one minute, Missy. I know Missah Kendall, he no easy man live with. He smart, he create. People that create, they a little strange."

Maddie burst out laughing, feeling giddy with a sudden case of nervous hysteria as the memory popped into her head of Robert describing Mrs. O'Malley as *strange*.

"It no joke!" Mrs. O'Malley insisted. "Right now, he need finish play. Lotsa trouble, lotsa worry. And, you ... you go through lotsa stuff too. Maybe you stay here couple more days, give another try. Then you and Missah Kendall get everything straight." She gave Maddie a soft smile. "Missah Kendall, he care for you. I know ... I *feel* it."

Maddie pondered the older woman's advice as she got up from the bed and reached under the night stand for her purse. As she opened the door, she looked over her shoulder. "Thanks for the use of your car. I promise to think about it."

* * * * *

Maddie closed the bedroom door behind her and headed for the stairs. She could hear the sound of voices coming. from the kitchen below. Imagining Robert had turned on the radio, Maddie stopped dead in her tracks the minute her foot hit the bottom step. What she saw pushed a gasp of horror out of her mouth as excruciating pain stabbed her chest.

Robert, seated at the breakfast table and wearing only a pair of raggy denim cutoffs, sipped coffee while Caesar lay stretched out on the floor beside him, eyes closed and snoring softly. Leaning across the table toward Robert with her back to Maddie sat a tall, fiery redhead. Without a doubt Maddie knew that woman was none other than the infamous Andrea – the source of the female voice she had assumed came from the radio. Her competition for Robert's affection sat only a few feet away and, for a split second, Maddie wanted to claw out the loathsome woman's overly-made up eyes. Knowing she couldn't stand there any longer, gaping at them like a fool, she decided to make a mad dash for Mrs. O'Malley's keys on the breadbox to her right. Trouble was, she couldn't seem to make herself move. Her feet felt glued to the floor.

Robert looked over at her and in a calm, casual manner said, "Good morning, Maddie. We've been waiting for you." She continued to stare at him, trying diligently to keep her anger in check.

Seeing her eyes blaze with fire, Robert knew that if looks could kill, he'd be a dead man. Without returning his greeting, she dashed for the breadbox, grabbed the keys, and ran for the door. But she wasn't fast enough. As if a bomb had gone off under him, he got to the door first.

Maddie made herself look up at him as he blocked her way out. It was painfully obvious that he had reached his breaking point. The tendons in his neck strained beneath his jaw, while a muscle twitched spasmodically in his cheek. But he said nothing. He just stood there and waited for her to speak. She took in a deep, unsteady breath. "Move!"

"Don't worry. I have no intention of stopping you." His face remained expressionless, but the acid tone of his voice made her wince as he ended, "But before you go, you need to know that in *this* house, guests are treated with courtesy and respect. Andrea came here this morning so that we can straighten out this matter, once and for all. The least you can do is say 'good morning' to her."

Maddie didn't budge. "Move!"

"Let her go, Robert," Andrea insisted, walking up behind Maddie. "Apparently, she's not interested in knowing the truth. Guess you've been wrong about her all along."

Incensed at the woman's audacity, Maddie spun around on her heels. "How dare you!"

"No," Andrea shot back. "How dare *you*! By the way you've been treating my friend, I'd say you *deserve* to lose him. If you won't trust him and won't listen to him when he tells you the truth straight to your face, then you don't deserve the truth, and he's better off without you."

That did it for Maddie. She pushed Robert to the side, opened the door, and ran from the house. Once inside Mrs. O'Malley's car, she sped off, brushing back tears of anger and hurt that refused to be held back.

* * * * *

Robert was buffing the hood of his car when Maddie pulled into the driveway. Mrs. O'Malley was standing beside him, her hands planted firmly on her hips. From the looks of things, Maddie realized she couldn't have returned at a more inopportune time. The housekeeper fired a litany of questions at him, her voice barely audible above the radio blaring from inside his car.

Turning off the ignition, Maddie slipped the newspaper under her arm, grabbed her purse, and stepped out of Mrs. O'Malley's white Toyota.

"You tell Missy 'bout tonight?" Mrs. O'Malley

bellowed, leaning over Robert to get his attention. Robert acted as if he didn't hear her. He turned his head and looked straight at Maddie.

Barely breathing, Maddie waited to hear his answer. He bit hard on his bottom lip, but said nothing. Maddie tensed up even more. *What about tonight?* What other surprise did he have in store for her? Could it be he was going out again with Andrea, which was why he was polishing his car with such enthusiasm? If that were the case, she didn't want to hear it. Not now. All she wanted to do was get out of her hot jeans and boots and into something cool and unrestricting.

She was just about to place the keys in Mrs. O'Malley's hand when Robert leaned against the brightly polished hood, crossed his legs at the ankles, and tossed the buffing cloth to her, giving a half-smile when she caught it.

"Have any luck?" he asked in a tone of indifference. Standing a mere three feet away, with his housekeeper standing between them, Maddie could smell him. The aroma of soap mingled with perspiration was tantalizingly male and earthly sensual. It was the same scent that filled her senses the previous afternoon on the beach when they were wrapped in each other's...

"Earth to Maddie," Robert quipped, his eyes fixed intently on Maddie's. *No*, he told himself. She wasn't going to leave him now, not after what Andrea had said. Left alone for a couple of hours, she'd had plenty of time to cool down and think things through ... unless...

"I hear you, Robert," she said blandly, "and, yes, I did have some luck. I found a place."

Robert felt the color drain from his cheeks. "Where?"

"In Plymouth."

"When will you be going?"

"Tonight."

"Tonight!" Robert took a step closer to her. "You ... ah ... you *can't* go tonight! I ... ah ... I mean, please don't go tonight. It's important you stay–"

"Please," Mrs. O'Malley interrupted, clasping the car keys tightly in her hand. "You promise to think 'bout it. You need stay."

"I gave it a lot of thought, Mrs. O'Malley. I really did. Thank you for the use of your car." With that, Maddie walked around the two, pitched the buffing cloth back to Robert, and went into the house.

* * * * *

Alone in her room, Maddie tossed the newspaper and purse onto the bed, then peeled off her clothes. Yesterday the temperature was a balmy seventy-five degrees. Today it had soared to the high eighties. Everyone she met was still dressed in shorts, sandals and sundresses. Clad in a turtleneck jersey, jeans and leather boots, she had felt like a fish out of water. She searched through her suitcase for her favorite tank top and lace bikini briefs. Just looking at them made her feel cooler already.

After slipping them on, Maddie went to the open French doors and gazed out on the ocean, watching the waves gently lap upon the shore. Ordinarily the gentle sound of the rolling tide had a calming, soothing affect on her. But not this time. Now it merely served as a backdrop for her thoughts, which should have been centered on her new residence – a simple room in a boarding house, which was a far cry from this lovely home. Instead, they were concentrated on Robert and his housekeeper and the reason for their wanting her to stay at the house tonight.

Drawing a blank, she turned to the bed where the newspaper lay open. Picking it up, she decided to call the number listed to confirm the room's availability. Since her room here at the house didn't have a telephone, and her cell phone had gotten lost when she was battling the storm, she was forced to use one of the other phones situated throughout the house.

Not wanting to roam about in her skimpy attire, she slipped a pair of jeans on over her briefs. With newspaper in hand, she marched down the carpeted hall. Halfway down the stairs, she heard the rustling sound of papers coming from Robert's office. He was undoubtedly working on the play. Disturbing him to place a personal call was out of the question, especially since the matter was in reference to her leaving.

She decided to use the phone in the kitchen. She dialed the number and was shocked to learn the room would not be available that evening as promised. She would have to wait until the following morning. Holding her anger in check, Maddie politely pointed out to the landlord that he had stated the room *was* ready for immediate occupancy. But the landlord babbled on in a frenzied manner about a plumbing problem that was being remedied even as they spoke. Nevertheless, it would still take hours for the job to be completed. Therefore, Maddie had no choice but to wait until morning before she was able to leave.

Placing the receiver back on the hook, Maddie pondered the unexpected news for a moment, finally deciding it was best not to tell Robert about it right away.

Unforgettable   Lucille Narcian

Not because he would be delighted to discover that her plans had gone awry again, but because she was interested to learn the mysterious reason behind his plea that she stay the night. Certainly, he was up to something outrageous, and by now she was burning with curiosity to find out what it was.

Turning to leave, she gave quick inspection around the spotless kitchen, noticing the clock on the wall above the counter top. It was past two o'clock, which meant Mrs. O'Malley was tucked away in her room with her Tiparillos and bottle of Old Grandad, absorbed in her soap operas.

Suddenly feeling lost in the huge house, Maddie gave a sigh as she slowly made her way up the stairs back to her room. *Might as well take a nap*, she thought. At least it would kill some time. As it was, the day seemed endless despite her stormy encounter with Robert and Andrea that morning, and her trip to the coffee shop where she had brunch while poring over the daily newspaper.

Just as she reached the top landing, Maddie heard muffled sobs coming from Mrs. O'Malley's room. Undecided as to whether or not she should intrude on the woman, she found herself stepping quietly to the door standing slightly ajar.

Maddie froze when the housekeeper shot her a sidelong glance and, to her surprise, motioned for her to enter rather than shooing her away. Maddie was reluctant to go in, because the glass of bourbon the woman was downing rapidly indicated she wasted no time drowning her sorrows in alcohol.

Expecting to be berated for spying on her, Maddie started to approach the back of the woman's chair but tensed and backed up. Standing against the door, twisting the newspaper in her hands, she anxiously eyed the woman who looked exceptionally tiny and fragile in her overstuffed chair. Her almond-shaped eyes were glued to the portable television set that rested on a roll away stand in front of her. Beside the chair stood a folding table supporting a box of tissues, an overflowing ashtray and, of course, the half-emptied bottle of liquor.

"Come, Missy," the woman slurred. A commercial flashed on the screen, drawing a deep sigh of relief from the woman. It was as though she could finally relax for a moment.

Still standing against the door, Maddie lifted her gaze from the pitiful scene before her and looked around the room. Unlike hers, it was much smaller, projecting an aura of warmth and intimacy with its white ruffled Priscilla curtains and blue patchwork quilt folded neatly at the bottom of the bed. On the nightstand beside the headboard sat an electric hurricane lamp and a yellowed, creased photograph in a small gold frame. Maddie was certain the man in the picture was Frank.

"No stand there, Missy. Come, sit."

Obediently, Maddie stepped around the woman and took a seat in the Boston rocker across from her. She didn't know how to express it properly, but realizing she was expected to explain her presence outside the housekeeper's room, she stammered, "I-I wasn't spying on you, Mrs. O'Malley. It's-it's just that I – uh – couldn't help but hear you weeping, and – uh – I was concerned that–"

"No need explain," the older woman cut in while she poured herself a refill. "Everyone on Cape know I drink. It no secret – or *why* I drink," she admitted. "It get me through day. Nighttime, I too tired to think 'bout Frank ... or *him*."

95

As ridiculous as it seemed, Maddie was genuinely moved by the woman's sorrow over the demise of the television star she seemed to worship. "I know that the man was your favorite actor," Maddie stated softly, feeling she had to say something – anything – to ease the woman's pain.

Out of the blue, Mrs. O'Malley's demeanor changed. She became outraged. "He look like my Frank, and make me remember my Frank! And now *he* gone too, like Frank!" The words trembled on her tongue, and her face crinkled. "How you know 'bout Leon, Missy?"

Stunned by the woman's angry outburst, Maddie blurted, "You told me. Don't you remember? It was yesterday. He had a heart attack on the show, and it devastated you. And he may be gone, but trust me, tomorrow he'll magically appear on another show, and you'll be able to fall in love with him all over again."

The housekeeper lowered her face into her hands, the wad of tissues she clutched practically covering her entire face. "I so sorry for way I act yesterday and today," she said, her words partly muffled by the tissues. "But Leon ... when he have heart attack, it hit too close to home. I lose control."

She dragged her trembling hands away and, holding her head high, looked Maddie straight in the eyes. "His death remind me when I lose Frank Three years ago Frank gone, but it seems like yesterday. Our time together so short."

She shook her head sadly. In retrospect, she managed to convey a little grin. "It love first-sight. I never believe 'til it happen to me." She turned her head and stared blankly at the television screen. "He not Chinese like me.

He Irish." She sat up straighter and pronounced, "Frances Sean O'Malley," as if it were an important declaration, then sighed and collapsed a little. "A beautiful name. A beautiful man. We so happy together. Then, just like that, he gone. Damn heart attack!" She her crumpled her tissue and swiped it across her eyes. "I rehearse for Missah Kendall play, never even get to say good-bye to him." Her eyes welled again with tears. "Now I got nothing – nothing but some memories and this job working for Missah Kendall."

At the mention of Robert's name, Maddie blushed crimson. It didn't go unnoticed by Mrs. O'Malley. "You love Missah Kendall," she said, wiping away the last of her tears.

The straightforward pronouncement caught Maddie off guard. Her heart began beating so rapidly, she couldn't respond. All she could do was look down at the newspaper folded in her lap.

"Yeah, I know," the older woman replied with the assurance of one who possessed a sixth sense when it came to matters of the heart. "I know he love you too."

At that, Maddie's head jerked up, and she glared at the Mrs. O'Malley. "You couldn't be more wrong."

The housekeeper half-smiled. "I got eyes. I see. All signs there."

Maddie drew in a shuddering breath. "I'm afraid you've missed your mark this time. Like I told you this morning, Mr. Kendall and I – well, we just don't see eye to eye. However, you and I have a great deal in common where Mr. Kendall is concerned. We were both rescued by him. He took you under his wing when you lost your husband. He rescued me from a torrential rain storm. My car was ruined beyond repair, and I was practically penniless. I had no one to turn to ... no place to go. Mr. Kendall took pity on me, brought me here and offered me a job typing his play, which I will still be doing, just not here in his office, but in my own room in a boarding house over in Plymouth." She rose to her feet and held out the circled ad in the newspaper for Mrs. O'Malley to see. "I was supposed to move in tonight, but there's a problem with the plumbing, so I have to wait until tomorrow morning."

The housekeeper bent forward in her seat, clutched the thick arm of her chair and replied brusquely, "Missy, you make big, big mistake if you go."

Maddie stood her ground and spoke what was in her heart. "No, I'm not making a mistake, Mrs. O'Malley. No matter what you say, I don't belong here. I ... I feel like an intruder. Mr. Kendall has his own life with his own friends and ... and..." The true reason stuck in her throat, and she was unable to verbalize it. "It's better I leave first thing tomorrow. And if you don't mind, I'd rather not discuss Mr. Kendall anymore."

The older woman flashed her dark eyes on Maddie. "You listen, Missy. You go, and you sorry rest of your life."

Maddie shifted nervously on her feet, wanting to hurry to the door and stop this line of conversation. But she couldn't resist hearing Mrs. O'Malley's side of it. "You keep telling me that. Why?"

"I tell you why. First day you come here, I see big change in Missah Kendall. He finally happy, even when you and him fight. The way he look at you..." Mrs. O'Malley shook her head with a wistful smile. "He even sing in shower. And he *never* ask me to make picnic lunch except for you. Now. You go, all that change. He turn into same old grumpy guy like before." She stopped talking long enough to finish the liquor that remained in her glass. "That Andrea lady break you two apart. I see that. But running away solve nothing."

The housekeeper had spoken with such an acute perception of the situation, that Maddie closed her eyes to keep back the tears. She looked away and replied somewhat exasperated, "Mr. Kendall is free to choose any woman he wants. I'm not blind, my friend. You may see the way he looks at me, but I see the way he looks at *her*. So we shared a picnic lunch together. So what? It hasn't changed a thing between them."

Mrs. O'Malley slammed her fist on the arm of her chair and shouted angrily, "There no *them,* I tell you! You the one he love. Tonight he prove me right. You see."

Maddie raised her eyes heavenward. First Robert made such a fuss about tonight, and now Mrs. O'Malley. What was going to happen tonight that would bring his love for her surprisingly to light?

Mrs. O'Malley quickly got to her feet and switched off the television. For a brief moment she paused and stared at the blank screen. Observing the woman with a keen eye, Maddie intuitively knew the housekeeper was either about to make a strong statement or ask a hard, direct question and was weighing her words carefully. When she finally turned to face her, Maddie noticed the cold, somber expression on her face. A frown drew her dark eyebrows together, narrowing her coal black eyes. From Maddie's viewpoint, they appeared like hooded slits, unseeing, yet able to look right through her.

"I know it not my business, but you tell me," the older woman demanded, shaking a scrawny veined finger at Maddie. "You love him?"

Not really wanting to answer the question, Maddie replied flatly, "Excuse me, Mrs. O'Malley, I don't mean to be impolite, but as you pointed out, that's none of your concern. Like you, I simply work for him. Only from now on I will be working elsewhere."

"I say before, and I say again," the older woman warned. "You a fool if you go! Two people love each other should stay together. Take it from me, old woman who know. I do anything for one more day with my Frank. So, you *no* love Missah Kendall, say so and I drop it. But you *do*, then I got a plan. No ask questions, just leave everything to me. When I done, Missah Kendall, he *beg* to marry you. *Tonight!*"

By this time, Maddie was so stunned by the housekeeper's certainty and forcefulness, she couldn't utter a sound. She just stood there wide-eyed, her mind in a whirl as she peered down at the woman who, at barely five feet tall, took command with the authority of one twice her size.

Mrs. O'Malley took Maddie by the arm and led her to the door. Opening it, she turned to Maddie and announced, "Today Missah Kendall forty birthday. Tonight he give fancy party, celebrate. *That* why he, and me too, we no want you leave tonight."

"But–"

"No *but*, Missy! You go to room and find prettiest dress you got." Mrs. O'Malley pressed a finger to her thin lips, then added, "You got a fancy dress, I hope."

"Yes," Maddie answered. "I have two, and they're still here." She shifted her gaze away from Mrs. O'Malley. Truth was, she had brought two gowns with her to dazzle Alex on their honeymoon.

"Great!" the housekeeper exclaimed in relief. "Now

go! You got plenty time relax, soak in tub, take nap. I go fix snack for you and Missah Kendall. I bet you both hungry."

There was silence for a moment, then Mrs. O'Malley's expression became somber again. "That woman with red hair come here this morning, see Missah Kendall. He ask me make coffee. I mad. Missah Kendall say it business. She no fool me. She want monkey business."

Maddie gave Mrs. O'Malley a coy little smile. "Sounds like you don't care for the lady."

The older woman gave a grunt. "She no lady. She ... uh-uh..." She fumbled for a moment to find the right word to describe her and, when she couldn't, simply blurted out, "She *different.* I never seen no woman like her. She hang around Missah Kendall like vulture, like she gonna dig her claws in him. I tell Missah Kendall watch out, she nothing but trouble, but he just laugh. We see tonight who gonna get last laugh!"

Mrs. O'Malley closed the door behind them. As they walked down the hall, she gave Maddie one last instruction. "You eat then get a nap, you hear me? You gotta be ready and look very, very beautiful when you come downstairs tonight. Eight o'clock sharp – you no be late!"

* * * * *

After Maddie finished her snack, she crawled into bed, gave a cat-like stretch, and fluffed up her pillow. A nap was just what she needed after the tense and exhausting day she'd had. She was just about to drift off when Andrea's scathing words attacked her brain like a jack hammer, causing her eyes to fly open. *You deserve to lose him. If you won't trust him and won't listen when he tells you the truth straight to your face, then you don't deserve the truth, and he's better off without you ... better off without you ... better off without–*

Maddie sat up with a start. Beads of perspiration dotted her brow, neck and torso. Throwing back the covers, she darted from the bed and ran into the bathroom. Grabbing a hand towel, she wiped her face, then took a cold, hard look at herself in the mirror. Was it possible that Andrea's accusations were true and that Robert *was* better off without her? Just thinking about a life without him made her grow weak in the knees. She dropped to the edge of the bathtub with a thud.

Was Mrs. O'Malley right? *Was* she being an idiot, running out on Robert? Did he really and truly love her? Sitting on the edge of the tub, she buried her face in her hands. She was so confused. Why would Andrea say something like that if she really wanted Robert for herself? Was she just trying to put more doubt into her and convince her she wasn't worthy of Robert?

Maddie lifted her head and shook herself clear of those doubts. It didn't matter what Andrea said. Robert had been about to tell her something, and she had simply run out on him, depriving him of the chance. And then when she'd returned, he'd been so cool toward her. Had her stubbornness caused her to lose the only man she truly did love?

She swiped a hand across her face and stood up from the tub. She didn't know whether Mrs. O'Malley was right about Robert loving her, or was simply deluding herself – as Maddie had been. *Was* Robert's love a delusion? He seemed so sincere, yet–

She groaned and marched back into her bedroom.

She'd just have to trust Mrs. O'Malley and wait until tonight to find out. It was her last – her only – chance to redeem herself with Robert and find out where she really stood with him.

CHAPTER EIGHT

*A*t ten minutes to eight, Maddie stepped before the full length mirror in her room and viewed her reflection with awe. Not only did she look radiant, she glowed with an aura of elegance and seductiveness. Just as she twirled to admire her image from all sides, Mrs. O'Malley flung open the door without bothering to knock first. Stopping dead in her tracks, she looked at Maddie and flashed a wide smile. "You beautiful," she breathed, giving Maddie a final inspection. "Missah Kendall not take eyes off you. Neither will guests."

"Thanks to you," Maddie replied gratefully. And it was true. The housekeeper had pressed her gown free of wrinkles and had applied her makeup with the expertise of an artist. But the *pièce de résistance* was not her gown or her makeup. It was her hair. Mrs. O'Malley had brushed it vigorously to a silky sheen, then coiled it intricately through itself at the back of her head until it cascaded in soft curls down Maddie's back. Then the housekeeper took her own strand of pearls and entwined them between the ringlets.

"Hair match gown perfectly," the older woman remarked. Maddie nodded in agreement as she admired her reflection in the mirror, noting how the strapless tight-fitting bodice studded with matching seed pearls accentuated the round swell of her breasts. The form-fitting gown of ice-blue satin matched the color of her eyes and made her creamy white skin dazzle.

Mrs. O'Malley smugly reinspected each ringlet and pearl, obviously thinking to herself that she had done a spectacular job – and Maddie agreed. When they both decided there was no need for jewelry, Maddie turned her gaze away from the mirror and slid her left leg slightly to the side. The skirt material parted gracefully, revealing her long, shapely leg. "Do you think the slit is too high?" she asked, knowing it was, and loving the delicious sexy feeling it gave her. "It practically shows my whole thigh."

"Designer intention," the housekeeper said, grinning wickedly. Soon, both of them were giggling like school girls.

Stepping over to the dresser, Maddie picked up her evening bag. "Well," she said excitedly, "I'm ready."

"Wait couple minutes," the older woman advised. "Need some men standing around bar in foyer. I hear whistles already. They make Missah Kendall very jealous." She and Maddie both laughed at that vision.

Mrs. O'Malley gave Maddie one last admiring glance, then turned to leave. "I do all I can. Now everything up to you. You really want Missah Kendall, go for it. You no can miss. Trust me." She was out the door before Maddie had a chance to thank her again.

Knowing she had to somehow convince Robert she was wrong about doubting him all along, she felt restless, excited, and nervous beyond words. While Mrs. O'Malley had been styling her hair, she'd assured Maddie she'd be the most desirable woman at the party. She had also responded *yes* when Maddie reluctantly asked if Andrea was going to attend the party tonight. The affirmation had brought an instant rush of anxiety that tightened Maddie's chest. Despite the housekeeper's tireless efforts to assure her that she would outshine every female there, Maddie couldn't help but wonder if she'd still pale next to Andrea.

Suppose the woman's hairdo was straight out of *Vogue* magazine, and her gown designed especially for this occasion? Suppose it was molded to her body with a bodice more revealing and more enticing, thus drawing the hungry eyes of the male guests to follow her with lustful stares? These were probabilities that hadn't entered Maddie's mind until now. For as sure as a full moon hung in the star-filled sky tonight, she was certain that Andrea was prepared to outdo every woman there. She'd see to it that each man would be panting over her, thus leaving Maddie to feel like Cinderella *before* the ball. Mrs. O'Malley reassured her everything would go according to plan, but still she felt uneasy.

Rechecking her makeup, hair, and gown in the mirror, Maddie never in her life had looked – *felt* – so beautiful. Her only hope was that Robert would think the same so that when she begged his forgiveness, he would certainly grant it to her. But with Andrea there, everything could turn out differently.

"Not a chance, *Red*," she said, suddenly filled with a burst of confidence as she viewed herself one last time in the mirror. Tonight belonged to her, and she willed herself to remove all negative thoughts that gnawed at her insides. Taking one last deep breath, she stepped to the door and opened it slightly. Hearing the distinctive rise and fall of voices below in the foyer, she decided to make her grand entrance.

Lifting the gown just high enough not to trip, Maddie descended the long staircase. By the time she reached the landing, total silence had permeated the foyer, then *ooohs*, and *aaahs* could be heard throughout the entire house.

To Maddie's delight, Robert was standing at the foot of the stairs. But when their eyes met and locked, she saw, to her dismay, that his face was expressionless. If he thought she looked beautiful, he certainly didn't show it the way he always did. His blank look of indifference made Maddie's heart sink.

Outstretching his hand, he slid hers in his, then guided her silently to the bar. When asked by the bartender what she would like to drink, she requested white wine. Obviously taken in by her beauty, along with the rest of the guests, the bartender practically spilled the wine all over himself. Beet red, he finally handed her the drink.

Robert lifted his glass, tapped it gently against hers, then turned and announced proudly to everyone, "My friends, I'd like to introduce you to Miss Maddie Price. Miss Price is assisting me with my new play, and I'm sure you'll all agree with me that her beauty makes my work both a pleasurable experience, and at the same time, a most difficult task."

The crowd chuckled heartily with some of the men giving a hearty pat on the back to Robert before continuing to scatter about with their partners. Ordinarily, such an introduction would have colored Maddie's cheeks a bright crimson. But this time, Robert's compliment had no effect on her. She was too busy scanning the guests, looking for Andrea. As Robert busied himself with his guests, she felt somewhat abandoned and distanced herself from him to make a more thorough search for her nemesis.

"She not here yet," Mrs. O'Malley whispered, instinctively reading Maddie's fear as she passed her in the foyer. Maddie, somewhat disappointed, turned slightly to see the housekeeper setting a tray of clean glasses on the bar. "No worry," the older woman muttered out of the corner of her mouth, "she gonna come. Probably not on time so she can make grand entrance."

"Will she be seated at the dinner table next to Mr. Kendall?" Maddie whispered back.
"No, no," the housekeeper answered, flashing her a bright smile. "Missah Kendall make seating arrangement himself. You sit on his right. His brother David sit on his left."

Perfect, Maddie thought to herself as she found Robert and boldly circled her arm around his, hoping he'd warm up to her. But he didn't. He casually removed her arm, took her by the hand, and guided her through the crowd. Maddie tried to hide her hurt and disappointment at his rejection by purposely flashing an extra warm smile to each guest who was now being personally introduced to her. However, their names escaped her the minute she walked away, for all she could think about were Andrea's words ... *you deserve to lose him*.

"I think you'd better sit before you fall down," Robert said blandly, interrupting her thoughts.

"What are you talking about?" she asked, giving him a wide-eyed look. "I'm fine."

"No you're not, you're a nervous wreck. Your nails are digging into my hand so tightly, it's about to bleed." He studied her closely, then queried in an angry tone, "It's still Andrea, isn't it?"

At the mention of the woman's name, Maddie

stopped short and looked soulfully into his eyes. "Please, Robert, let's sit on the sofa for just a minute, please. I know you're angry with me, and I can't bear it any longer. You deserve an apology for the despicable way I've been behaving, not only this morning, but every time you've pleaded with me to *trust* you – to – *believe* that you and Andrea are nothing more than friends. Well, I do believe you and I'm sorry–"

Just then, Maddie's apology was interrupted by the waiter who came and stood before them with a tray of fresh drinks. Robert got them both a refill, then ushered her to the sofa in the living room. He had just settled down beside her when Maddie put the question to him. "Will you ever forgive me for doubting you?"

For a long, heart-stopping moment of silence, Robert merely looked down at her. Then he lowered his face so close, she could feel his hot breath on her mouth. "Of course I forgive you, sweetheart. Now let's put this silly misunderstanding behind us and enjoy the party." Pulling her even closer, he murmured in her ear, "God, Maddie, you're simply breathtaking."

That was all Maddie needed to hear. Relief flooded her insides. She wasn't going to lose him after all. The realization set her free. Her self-confidence returned, and she became playful. Taking a tiny sip of wine, she purposely crossed her long legs in front of Robert, who couldn't help but watch as the material parted, revealing a generous portion of her thigh. His desire for her was painfully visible in his eyes as they traveled her entire body.

"Breathtaking," he repeated again. "Simply breathtaking."

Maddie smiled coyly at him, then turned her gaze to

the contents of her glass. "Mrs. O'Malley deserves all the credit," she confessed. "She did my hair and makeup. She even pressed my gown. I don't know what I would have done without her."

"I must remember to slip a bonus in her check this week for doing an outstanding job," he answered, "although even if you had worn your jeans and a sweatshirt with your hair twisted in braids, you'd still be the most beautiful woman here. I can't tell you how proud I am to be your escort."

This time his compliment brought a bright blush to her cheeks and a slight tremble to her hands. She was painfully conscious of his searing eyes upon her. They seemed to be peeling the gown from her body, making her feel naked and fully exposed to the room full of people.

"Stop it," she whispered harshly. "You're embarrassing me."

Robert leaned closer and whispered in her ear, "And you're loving every minute of it."

"You're right," she admitted, "but put your eyeballs back in your head. You're attracting too much attention. People are beginning to stare."

"Let them," he replied, while his thumb traced the smooth outline of her jaw. His touch sparked the memory of their lovemaking on the beach, and she trembled, recalling how it had left her mindless.

"Everyone's fascinated by you, Maddie," Robert whispered in her ear. "Can't say I blame them. As a matter of fact, why don't we go out on the patio so we can spend a few minutes alone? I'm dying to kiss you. I *need* to kiss you. You're driving me mad."

She was just about to answer when the sound of a

woman's voice coming from the foyer attracted her attention. Maddie's heart skipped a beat. With a calm voice that belied the quivering in her stomach she said, "And miss Andrea's grand entrance? She's standing in the doorway looking straight at you. Now, be a good host and invite her to join us."

At the suggestion, Robert turned in the woman's direction and smiled.

* * * * *

In a world saturated with beautiful women, Andrea definitely stood out from the crowd. Impressively tall even without the added height provided by the stiletto heels she wore, Andrea was dressed in a high-necked, emerald green beaded gown that left little to the imagination. A white mink stole was casually draped over one shoulder, and her signature flaming red hair hung long and loose, framing her perfect oval face. Even at this distance, Maddie could see that Andrea's hazel green eyes rimmed by long sooty lashes remained focused on Robert.

And the manner in which she carried herself certainly could not be overlooked. Her demeanor commanded attention, which she seemed to enjoy to the fullest. It apparently gave her a feeling of dominance – of power that permeated the room. She had *presence* and *magnetism,* and for certain no one at that moment felt it more than Maddie.

"You really don't mind if I ask her to join us?" Robert asked, bringing Maddie out of her musings.

Her heart leaped into her throat. "Of course not," she answered, her voice cracking with nervousness. "It would be very impolite of you if you didn't."

"You really mean that?"

"Of course," Maddie replied, feigning an air of cool indifference. Truth was, with her eyes transfixed on Andrea, Maddie felt her self-confidence take a nose dive. She knew the woman was stunning, but tonight she was drop-dead gorgeous. Maddie tried not to allow any hint of jealousy to creep into her voice as she urged, "Hurry, Robert, can't you see she's waiting?"

Robert swallowed the remainder of his drink in one swift gulp, then practically laughed as he said, "You finally figured out what I've been trying to tell you all along!"

Still clueless, Maddie glanced back at Robert, trying to judge his eagerness to be with Andrea. He didn't seem *that* interested, so she persisted, "Go on. Go on."

"Women," he groaned, as he rose to his feet. "Try and figure them." He pasted a smile on his face and waved Andrea over to the sofa."

Maddie's glare grew colder as she watched the statuesque woman thread her way through the crowd. When she reached the sofa, she slithered down next to Maddie. Keeping her green-eyed gaze fixed on her, Andrea ordered Robert to bring her a double scotch on the rocks. As soon as Robert left, Andrea leaned back against the soft sofa pillows and crooned, "From the looks of things, I gather you thought about what I said this morning and apologized to Robert. I'm glad you finally came to your senses." She tapped Maddie lightly on the arm. "By the way, you truly are a knockout."

"Thanks for the compliment," Maddie replied with a fake smile while shifting uncomfortably in her seat.

"It's not a compliment, honey," Andrea returned

almost breathlessly. "It's the truth."

From out of the blue, Maddie went cold all over. She couldn't help but notice the woman seemed to be undressing her with her eyes, the same way Robert's had. It shocked Maddie, and she suddenly wished Robert would hurry back. It was one thing to be looked at seductively by a man, but by a woman?

Relieved to find Robert suddenly standing before them, Maddie looked at him oddly as he handed Andrea her drink. Robert immediately sensed that something had transpired between the two while he was gone and, whatever it was, it had distressed Maddie immensely. Moreover, he couldn't make any inquiries because too many people were now standing within ear shot, and anything said would not be confidential.

All he could do at the moment was get Maddie away from Andrea. He would deal with the matter later when he could get her alone. Clearing his throat in an effort to calm himself, he announced, "Dinner is about to be served."

Thankful to have been rescued from this strange woman, Maddie got to her feet and felt Robert's gentle hand securely at her waist.

When Andrea rose from the sofa, she openly planted a light peck on Robert's cheek. "Happy Birthday, darling," she cooed, loud enough for everyone to hear. "And may you get everything in life you not only want, but truly deserve."

"Thanks pal, I'll get you for this," he mumbled beneath his breath when he saw several women giggling at Andrea's open display of affection. Unfortunately, Maddie heard him.

What is going on here? Maddie wondered, looking suspiciously at both of them. For such intimate friends, the tension between them now was thick enough to cut with a knife.

Jealousy. That's what this was all about, Maddie concluded. Robert wasn't paying enough attention to Andrea, and the woman obviously didn't like it one bit. An amused, almost wicked smile appeared on Maddie's face. This was going to be one hell of an evening after all.

* * * * *

Upon entering the dining room, an actor friend of Robert's, who was assuming the role of butler for the party, personally escorted the guests to their seats. A tall, thin man with wire-framed glasses and a short, thin mustache, he remained unmoved when Andrea balked that she didn't wish to be seated at the opposite end of the table, so far away from Robert. Maddie lowered her gaze to her lap and smiled slightly when Robert ignored Andrea's protests and seated her next to him. Knowing that if looks could kill she would be fatally wounded, Maddie didn't dare look over at the woman.

"And who is *this* gorgeous creature, Bobby old boy? I don't believe we've been introduced."

To Robert, there was no mistaking that familiar deep voice. Turning his head to the side, he laughed heartily while vigorously shaking the hand of the man who stood beside him. Maddie gave a long look at the man whose rugged jaw, full sensuous lips, and penetrating eyes confirmed her belief that he could be non other than Robert's brother, David.

At first, Robert assumed David was referring to Maddie. But when he saw his brother's smiling gray eyes fixed directly on Andrea, Robert went sick inside. *Good God*, he thought. *Why didn't I take him aside at the bar when I had the chance to warn him about Andrea?* But the fact was, Robert had been so intent on keeping Maddie here tonight that he completely forgot about David. He *had* made a mental note to explain the situation to his brother prior to calling him. But once they became engrossed in their conversation, the subject of the vivacious redhead never came up. Now he'd have to wait until after dinner to take David aside and clue him in. Which wasn't going to be easy. After all, how do you tell a man who's suddenly captivated by a gorgeous woman that she's not...

"Okay, big brother," David announced, taking Andrea's hand in his, "if you won't do the honors, then I'll just have to introduce myself."

Before Robert had a chance to utter a sound, David brushed a quick kiss on Andrea's hand and practically purred, "How do you do, pretty lady. I'm David, Robert's brother. And you must be the infamous Maddie Price. I must say, Robert didn't exaggerate one bit when he told me how lovely you are."

Maddie's lips twisted in amusement. This night was getting better by the minute. Or was it? To Maddie's chagrin, she noticed the color drain from Robert's face. Speechless, he just stood there watching Andrea bat her long, sooty eyelashes and flash David her sexiest smile. Finally, the woman purred back. "Sorry to disappoint you, darling, but I'm not Maddie. I'm Andrea. And I can't tell you how pleased I am to meet *you*."

"Excuse me, Miss," the butler interrupted, looking at Andrea. "If you'll follow me, I'll take you to your seat so that I may begin serving."

Keeping his gaze fixed on Andrea, David replied, "Thank you, but *I'll* escort the lady to her seat." With a light touch of his hand on her elbow, he led Andrea to her place at the far end of the table. Once she was seated, Robert noticed David whisper something in her ear. Whatever he said brought a smile and an immediate blush to Andrea's cheeks.

All the while, Maddie's eyes never left Robert. It was impossible to ignore the muscle that twitched angrily in his cheek or his hand which was now gripping the tablecloth in a valiant effort to control himself.

Inwardly furious over Robert's reaction to the couple who were carrying on like star-crossed lovers, Maddie couldn't bear to be near him another minute. She had to leave ... *now!* There was no need to question his obvious jealousy towards the couple. It was written all over his face. He *was* in love with Andrea, and that talk about her being nothing more than a friend was bull. As for Maddie, she was not about to continue watching this scene any longer.

Acting as casual as possible, she merely smiled at Robert and politely excused herself. Taking care not to arouse his or the guests suspicions that anything was wrong, she moved slowly towards the kitchen. Once inside, she marched to the telephone, thankful that Mrs. O'Malley was not in there puttering about. She was in no mood for explanations of any kind.

With a swift hand, she grabbed the phone book on the counter and flipped through the pages, stopping at the listings for taxis. When she located the one nearest to the house, she dialed the number. The dispatcher barely had a chance to speak before Maddie announced that this was an emergency, and could he send a car out immediately. She gave him the address and stated in no uncertain terms that the driver was not to sound the horn. She would be waiting in the driveway. Now all she had to do was get to her room unnoticed. She peeked out the kitchen door and gave a sigh of relief. Everyone was engrossed in conversation. Mrs. O'Malley and the butler were busy serving the hors d'oeuvres, their backs to her.

Running on tiptoes, she dashed up the stairs, entered her room, and grabbed her regular purse from the dresser drawer. There was no time to pack the rest of her clothes or retrieve her jacket from the closet in the foyer. Taking one last look around her room, she flicked away a falling teardrop, muttered an unladylike like oath, then flung open the French doors. Flying down the veranda steps, she had just made her way to the driveway when the taxi rolled up. Throwing open the door, she quickly slid inside. Heaving a sigh of relief at her successful mission, she reached over to close the door, only to see Caesar galloping towards her. His barking pierced the night like a cannon.

Maddie shut the door and leaned forward in her seat. "Hurry, driver."

CHAPTER NINE

$\mathcal{J}$ust before the last turn to the rooming house, Maddie noticed a dim light coming from a diner on the corner. Since she hadn't stayed for dinner at Robert's, her stomach growled for food, even though she had no appetite at all. As the driver approached the diner, Maddie asked him to stop and wait. Once inside, she headed for the counter, uncaring that the patrons scattered about had stopped talking and turned their heads her way. Without bothering to look at the menu displayed high on the wall, she ordered a large black coffee and an apple Danish to go. As she left the diner, she looked up at the starry sky. It was such a beautiful night, she decided to forgo the taxi and walk the short distance to the boarding house.

As soon as she opened the door to her room, Maddie's heart sank. "What a dump," she mumbled to herself, recalling the elegance of Robert's house. There were no gold satin drapes on her windows; no polished hardwood floors beneath her feet; no freshly painted walls ... and most of all, no one to talk to. Compared to the dinner music that played softly in the background at Robert's house while the guests conversed with each other, the quiet that surrounded her now was almost deafening. She hadn't taken all this into account when she made her hasty decision to leave the party. All she knew was that she couldn't bear to sit beside Robert another minute and watch in silence while he glared at his brother slobbering over Andrea.

That heart-breaking scene continued to play over and over in Maddie's mind as she sat down at her tiny kitchen table to drink her coffee. Still not hungry, she pushed the Danish aside, wiped a lonely teardrop from her cheek, then bent down and removed her shoes. Exhausted from the events of the day, and devastated by the night that had held such promise but ended up a living nightmare, she quickly undressed, removed Mrs. O'Malley's pearls from her hair, donned her pajamas, and crawled into bed.

She had hoped sleep would come fast ... a dreamless sleep where, for a few blessed hours, she would feel nothing but peace. Her tortured mind and broken heart needed precious time to forget and heal. She didn't want to think about Andrea, or Mrs. O'Malley, or Robert ... sweet Robert, who was now lying beneath her, unfastening the hook on her halter top while the warm September sun shone brightly above them.

"God, how I love you, Maddie," he groaned against the nape of her neck "I love the feel of you ... the taste of you in my mouth, so soft and sweet," he whispered lowering his head to her breast, then covering the sensitive peak with his lips. When he drew it in deeper, Maddie shuddered uncontrollably, and her legs parted to receive him. His lips continued to drive her wild, refusing to release their hold on her, even as he rolled her onto her back.

Maddie rolled her head from side to side, afraid to open her eyes ... afraid he'd be gone if she did. But when she felt him enter her hard and swift, she opened them wide and smiled.

Robert's face was above hers now, and she could see by the glazed look in his eyes that he was ready to explode, and so was she. When it erupted, he dug his fingers hard into her bare bottom and looked deeply into her eyes. "You're mine now ... *mine* ... do you hear? From now on we're a team. We're hot together ... so hot..."

"So hot," Maddie moaned, kicking off the covers. So hot. It was almost like the sun was directly over her, causing her to sweat profusely. But when she finally opened her eyes, she didn't see the glare of the sun, in fact, she couldn't see anything through the fog. *Fog*? "That isn't fog," she gasped realizing what it was. "It's *smoke*!"

Instinct told her to get out of the house immediately. Without stopping to put on her robe, slippers, or grab for her purse, she threw open the front door, only to have thick, dark clouds of smoke envelop her like a shroud. Her eyes began to burn, and she started to cough uncontrollably, yet she kept telling herself not to panic. She mustn't panic. There were two flights of stairs to go down before she would reach the outside door. If she froze with fear now, she would surely burn to death.

Sliding her hand along the banister, she fumbled her way barefoot down the steps yelling "Fire! Fire, everybody! Wake up! Wake up!" She banged on each door as she approached it, hoping to alert the occupants before the flames and the smoke claimed them. Flinging their doors open, the other tenants joined her, coughing and clambering their way through the halls and down the stairs until they reached the bottom floor. Behind the last apartment door, Maddie could hear a woman screaming.

With one swift turn of her hand, she unlocked the deadbolt on the outside door, pulled it open, and shoved the traumatized tenants within her reach out onto the porch. Pure terror raging inside her, she inhaled a huge gulp of air, gathered all the strength she had, and slammed her left shoulder hard against the apartment door, but it wouldn't budge.

"Help me! Help *me*!" she screamed at two of the male tenants who were pulling at each other to see who would make his way out of the building first. Cursing at the top of their lungs, the men stopped feuding when they heard Maddie's screams, went back and formed a human barrier with her. After taking a few steps back, the three charged forward into the door with their shoulders, splitting the wooden door open. The back-draft from the rush of air caused the smoke to obscure her view entirely. Fearing she had run out of time, Maddie screamed, "Where are you? Can you hear me?" Miraculously, a tiny ray of light swept across the woman who was crouched down under the kitchen table. She was holding a limp baby in her arms and wailing, "*I can't wake her up! I can't wake her up! Help me! Please help me!*" The flames were beginning to circle around them. In a minute, they'd all be trapped inside. Maddie snatched the baby from her mother's arms, and burying her tiny head into her breast, she ran out into the cool night air, while the men helped the distraught mother to safety.

Planked on the sidewalk, Maddie was giving the child mouth to mouth resuscitation when the first fire engine and ambulance arrived. A parade of others followed behind them. Maddie was crying and breathing furiously into the child's mouth when a fireman took the baby from her arms. "Please make her be alive," Maddie begged. " Don't leave until I know she's alive. Please!"

The ambulance driver joined the firefighter and, hovering over the child, he placed an oxygen mask over her tiny face. Meanwhile, stretchers were rolling up onto the sidewalk to take the tenants to the hospital, but Maddie didn't notice who needed help and who didn't. She was too busy praying. Just as an EMT strapped the child onto a stretcher, the little girl began to cry and cough. It was the most beautiful sound Maddie had ever heard. Overcome with joy and exhaustion, Maddie dropped down onto the sidewalk curb and sobbed.

By now, the street was filled with curiosity seekers, boarding house tenants, policemen and firefighters. Ambulances came and went. Even the press was on hand. An EMT insisted she go to the hospital, but Maddie refused. "I'm okay, really. I'm fine. Thank you."

Two hands reached out to her from the crowd. One hand held a bottle of water. The other, a face cloth and towel. "Here, take these."

"Thanks," she said, gulping down the water.

"Don't mention it," the voice replied. Maddie didn't have to look at the Good Samaritan to know it was Robert. Neither did she raise her eyes to look at him. "Go home, Robert, the crisis is over."

"I'm not leaving here without you."

"Wrong again, lover boy. Go home and take care of your own crisis. You're not wanted or needed here."

Dozens of firemen were leading the crowd on the sidewalk away from the building. She could feel the heat from the fire on her back, while the water from the hoses rained upon her from all directions. Maddie was wiping her face with the towel when it was immediately replaced with a microphone. "I'm Carla Reynolds from WBZTV Channel 4 in Boston. Are you all right, Miss?"

"Yes, thank you. I'm fine." Maddie answered through coughing spasms.

"Would you mind telling me your name?"

"Her name is Madelyn Price," Robert chimed in, pulling her to him. Maddie tried to free herself from Robert's strong embrace, but Caesar placed himself against her legs so that she couldn't move. The microphone switched from Maddie to Robert. "Are you the lady's husband?" the reporter asked gently.

Robert wished he could answer yes. Instead he uttered a nervous "No, I'm the lady's employer."

"And you are, sir?"

"Robert Kendall."

The reporter's eyes widened. "You mean *the* Robert Kendall? The famous playwright?"

"Yes," he answered flatly. "Now if you'll excuse us, I'm taking the lady home with me. She needs to rest and recoup."

Maddie opened her mouth to protest, but Robert shoved the face cloth into it then gathered her up into his arms and headed for his truck. Once inside, Maddie hissed, "What the hell do you think you're doing?"

"Taking you back where you belong," he said, maneuvering the truck free from the crowded street. Maddie became belligerent. "I *was* where I belong. Now, turn this bloody truck around and take me back. I'd rather do battle with the fire in my house than deal with the nuts in yours!"

"Now, now, Maddie," he said, keeping his voice calm. "You've been through one helluva night. All I want you to do is–"

"Knock it off!" she fired back at him. "I'm sick and

tired of hearing about what *you* want me to do! Just because you've rescued me for a second time doesn't mean I'm your–" The words stuck in her throat. Too upset and exhausted to go on, Maddie's eyes slowly closed and her head fell listlessly onto Robert's shoulder.

* * * * *

Mrs. O'Malley was standing in the open doorway when the truck pulled into the driveway. Leaving the doors open so she could get plenty of air, Robert gently lifted Maddie's unconscious body up into the circle of his arms and carried her into the house.

"Quick! Bring her to living room," the housekeeper ordered. "I open all windows."

"Then call Walter, Mei-Lin," Robert instructed, "and pray that he's home. If he's not, tell his answering service or whoever answers that his friend Bob is calling, and that I need him to come here right away. It's an emergency."

While Mrs. O'Malley tended to her duties, Robert placed Maddie gently on the living room sofa. From the soft light emitted by the two lamps that flanked the couch, it was painfully obvious to him the horror that Maddie had endured, saving the lives of her neighbors, especially the infant girl. He could only imagine the emotional trauma that went with it. As for the heartbreak she surely suffered at his hands during the dinner, Robert couldn't bear to think about it. Guilt-ridden and broken-hearted, he fell to his knees beside Maddie and sobbed bitter tears.

It was the first time since his wife died that Mrs. O'Malley had witnessed such intense emotion from him. Swallowing back tears of her own, she set a basin of soapy warm water, a face cloth and towel she was carrying, down on the coffee table, then knelt on the floor beside him.

"Look what I've done, my friend," he said in a strangled voice. "It's all my fault."

"No," she answered flatly. "Hussy friend to blame, too. Take good look at what you two do to poor Missy and tell me Andrea worth it," she spat out. "Then do me favor and take your guilty conscience somewhere else. I can only handle one patient at a time. I called doctor. He on his way."

* * * * *

"Good God, what happened?" Robert's friend asked, his eyes shifting from Maddie to Robert. Without waiting for an answer, the doctor went over to the couch and placed his medical bag on the coffee table.

Mrs. O'Malley was wiping Maddie's face gently with the wet face cloth. When the doctor placed his stethoscope on her chest, Maddie opened her eyes. Peering at him intently, she croaked, "I'm fine, doc." She swallowed and ignored the scratchiness of her raw throat. "All I need is a bath and a good night's sleep."

The doctor gave a slight grin and shook his head. "I'm afraid you need more than that, young lady. You're not fine. Are you able to tell me what happened to you?"

"You want the whole story or the condensed version?" Maddie quipped sarcastically, then coughed before she glared up at Robert.

"Take you're pick. I'm in no rush."

"I was in my room, sleeping, when–"

"Where *is* your room?" the doctor interrupted.

"In Plymouth," she answered. "Why?"

125

Walter gave an odd look. "Because you've obviously been in a fire, and there's been no report of one in this area tonight. Since Plymouth is quite a distance away, how did you happen to end up here?"

Not wanting Maddie to cough and irritate her parched throat even more, Robert asked her if he could fill in the details.

"Be my guest," she answered, her voice void of emotion.

Robert perched himself on the arm of the over-stuffed chair, his eyes never leaving hers. "Mrs. O'Malley and I were cleaning up after a dinner party tonight, when she heard the police scanner in my office blaring something about a fire in a rooming house in Plymouth. Miss Price is my secretary, and happens to live in that house. So, I immediately jumped into my truck and drove out there to make sure she was unhurt. When I arrived, I saw her sitting on the sidewalk curb, desperately breathing life into a dying child. She refused to budge until she knew the fate of the infant. She also refused to go to the hospital, and yet it was plain to see she needed medical help and also a place to stay until she's able to go back there ... *if* she's able to go back there. The damage is pretty extensive."

He paused and took an unsteady breath. "How is she, Walter? Be straight with me. Does she really need to go to the hospital?"

The doctor sighed heavily while checking Maddie over. "Her shoulder and left arm are pretty badly bruised. I honestly don't know how she didn't break them both. And her feet are in bad shape. There isn't any glass in them that I can find, but they're pretty badly cut up and swollen. She needs to be off them for at least a week."

126

He raised his eyes to Mrs. O'Malley, who was clutching some crystal rosary beads tightly in her hands. "Well, Mei-Lin, would you be up to taking care of this young lady for about a week? She'll require complete bed rest. That means meals in her room and sponge baths instead of a shower. The only time she can walk on her feet is to use the bathroom, and that's *if* she has a pair of thick-soled, very soft slippers."

Mei-Lin was thrilled that Maddie was not severely burned or maimed in the fire, and that she would be staying at the house for at least another week. As for running up and down the stairs all day to tend to the young girl's needs, she decided to delegate that job to Robert as part of his punishment for causing her to not only be inconvenienced, but for burdening Maddie with more undeserved grief and pain. The housekeeper gave Maddie a warm smile and said, "I happy take care of her. She absolute sweetheart."

"If she works for Robert, she must be a saint," the doctor said in jest as he removed his prescription pad, a needle and a bottle from his bag. "I'm going to give her a shot for the pain and want her to start on this antibiotic first thing tomorrow morning." He handed the paper to Robert, gave her the shot, then asked if she had any questions.

Maddie jumped right in. "Yes, I have. I need a shower desperately. I reek from soot and smoke. I don't have any pain now that you gave me the shot. Please say it's okay to take this one quick shower and shampoo."

He was just about to answer her when Mrs. O'Malley assured him that she would help Maddie get cleaned up and settled into bed.

"Okay, but just this once," the doctor replied. "I'll check in on you in about a week."

CHAPTER TEN

$\mathcal{M}$addie refrained from looking or speaking to Robert as he carried her up the stairs to her room. Yet, she acknowledged inwardly how wonderful it felt to be back in his arms again, even though she wanted to strangle him. She couldn't help but think it ironic she'd returned to the scene of the crime – that very same night, and didn't find Andrea there. Curious as to the whereabouts of the dazzling redhead, she said with all the sarcasm she could muster, "I don't see Miss Femme Fatale floating around on her broom. Did you hide her under the sink with the Drano?"

"Now, now, Maddie, don't be caustic," Robert answered, trying hard to keep from laughing. Even cut and bruised, she still managed to keep her sense of humor.

The doors to her room and bath were open. Mrs. O'Malley was waiting by the shower with some fresh towels and a nightgown that was obviously too small for Maddie. Robert set her down on the soft rug and said he'd be back later to say goodnight.

Once she was in the shower, the older woman gave Maddie a full inspection. "Good lord, Missy," she gulped, the sight of the cuts and bruises pulling at her heart strings. "I never see bruises like this before. Maybe you *should* go to hospital. You sure you okay?"

"With you looking after me, I'll be as good as new before you know it. Now, please give my hair a good scrubbing."

Ordinarily, Maddie loved to linger in the shower, relishing the way the warm water floated over her delicate skin, but not tonight. The water felt like shards of glass digging into her bruised shoulder and arm that were now turning black and blue, then down to her cut and swollen feet, making her want to scream. "Please, no more," Maddie pleaded. "I've had enough."

Wrapping the young girl ever so gently in the towels, the housekeeper led her to her bed. Flinging back the covers, she said, "Lay down straight. I pat you dry. I have burn ointments in medicine cabinet and gauze pads. I get them." When she returned, she tended to Maddie as one would a delicate wounded bird. When she picked up the nightgown, she couldn't help but chuckle. "This mine, too small, but will do for tonight. Tomorrow I go shopping. Get everything you need." She tucked Maddie in and stated she'd return with a hair dryer and a cup of hot tea.

"And a few of your wonderful sugar cookies?" Maddie suggested, giggling. The older woman gave her a smile and a peck on her brow, then left the room.

Returning shortly with a hairdryer and Maddie's snacks, Mei-Lin dried her hair and could see the exhaustion in Maddie's face. "Rest now," she whispered softly when she was through. "You need me, you call me. I hear you." Walking on tiptoes, she turned off the lamp and left the room.

* * * * *

129

A gentle breeze and a soft ray of light from the full moon shone through the sheer curtains on the open French doors, casting dancing shadows on the walls and a warm glow across her bed. Maddie remembered how much she had fallen in love with this room the first time she saw it. Now, she looked upon it as a beautifully decorated prison cell where she was now confined to her bed, unable to come and go as she pleased. And all because of a bloody flat tire ... and a sultry siren named Andrea.

She was on the brink of falling asleep when she heard a light rapping on the door. It wasn't necessary to ask who it was. Head bowed low, Robert entered the room and stepped to the side of her bed. Maddie opened her eyes and looked at him but said nothing. Robert finally broke the silence. "I'm sure you must be quite uncomfortable in Mei-Lin's nightgown, so I brought you one of my pajama tops. At least it's big and roomy and ... oh, God, Maddie," he choked. "Will you ever forgive me for putting you through hell tonight and every other..."

"No more, Robert," she breathed, fighting back the pain of wanting him that tore at her heart. "I'm too exhausted to talk about anything tonight. Maybe tomorrow." Before he had a chance to answer, she threw off the covers. "Please get me out of this nightgown," she pleaded. "It's so tight it feels like a straightjacket, especially around my arms."

"Perhaps you'd be more comfortable if Mei-Lin helped you instead of me," he replied, knowing that if he saw her naked, bruised body it would destroy him completely.

She looked at him with liquid blue eyes that bore into his very soul. "No. Let her rest. She's exhausted."

He gave a cursory glance at the nightgown. It was an old, faded cotton thing that had seen better days. It clung to her like a second skin. "The only way to remove it, Maddie," he said gently, "is to cut or tear it off. If I try to lift it over your head, you'll be in excruciating pain."

"I don't care how you do it," she replied flatly. "Just get it off me."

Robert wasted no time in removing the offending garment. He placed both hands at the neckline and gave a hard tug. The material parted easily beneath his fingers. The sight of her milky white breasts made him grow hard, so he crossed his legs to hide his arousal. But he wasn't fast enough. Even in the fleeting rays of the moonlight, Maddie could see her effect on him. Automatically, her nipples swelled in response. For some insane reason, the hurt and humiliation he had put her through in the past few hours quickly vanished, and no matter how hard she tried to put her feelings for him aside, it was futile to ignore or deny how much she loved him.

Knowing what he had to do next would require every ounce of emotional strength he could muster. He swallowed a hard gulp and asked, "Are you able to sit up?" Looking deeply into his eyes, Maddie nodded, yes. "Good. Now lean against me and I'll roll the sleeves down gently. Then you'll be able to slip my pajama top on easily."

Although he had shaved earlier that night, his beard had grown enough so that Maddie could feel it against her cheek. The brackets on each side of his mouth framed the magnificent cut of his lips, and she couldn't help remembering the way he had closed those lips over her nipples on the beach, sucking her tender flesh into his mouth. She quivered, and the rigidity went out of her body.

131

He gently removed the nightgown, then carefully replaced it with his roomy pajama top.

As he buttoned each button, he could feel beads of perspiration begin to cover her brow and cheeks. Reaching into the back pocket of his jeans, he quickly withdrew his handkerchief. With a measured look he asked, "Are you in pain?"

"No," she whispered and reached for the handkerchief.

"Let me do it," he breathed, slowly drawing the cloth over her delicate features. He wiped her mouth with a touch so light, she barely felt it, then watched the cloth as it tugged slightly at her soft, enticing lower lip.

Without conscious effort, Maddie tilted her head back and closed her eyes. Robert continued to draw the handkerchief down her throat and into the loose neck of her top. At this point she should have told him to stop, but she didn't want him to. Her breath caught at the exquisite feel of the cloth that was now skimming her nipples, keeping them at attention. They began to throb, and she arched her back involuntarily, offering them for more. He moved closer and she could feel him growing, pressing against her, as her blood flowed heavily through her veins.

He tossed the handkerchief onto the bed. The arm behind her back tightened just enough to draw her to him even closer, as he bent his head and closed his mouth over hers. Catching himself, he lifted his head and, on a labored breath, whispered, "I'm sorry, honey. Guess I got carried away. I don't want to hurt you."

"You're not hurting me," she whispered back, then drew him down to her. His mouth was hard and hot and urgent in his demands. His tongue pushed into her mouth, and she met it with her own, welcoming it, wanting more. He slid her back down gently on the bed and kissed her once again while he put his hand beneath the pajama top and closed it over her breast. He kneaded the firm mound gently, rubbing his smooth palm over the nipple until she whimpered into his mouth from the exquisite pain of it. Turning slightly, she lifted her unbruised arm and wound it around his neck. Excitement pounded in the pit of her stomach, tightening every muscle in her body until she could feel an aching tension between her legs.

With a rough groan of passion, he bent her back over his arm and shoved the pajama top up, exposing her breasts to him again. His warm breath feathered across them as he bent to her, then he extended the tip of his tongue and circled one pink nipple, making it constrict into a tightly puckered nub.

Maddie clutched at him. "Please, Robert," she begged in a low shaking voice. This was the hot magic – the same warm promise she had felt lying beneath him on the beach, and she wanted more. He drew her nipple into his mouth with a strong, sucking pressure, and she arched again at the exquisite sensations.

With an effort that brought sweat to his brow, he suddenly lifted his mouth from her sweet flesh and got to his feet. At first she swayed, then with dazed eyes, she looked down at her naked breasts. She didn't understand what had just happened, so she reached for him, offering a drugging sensuality that he couldn't let himself take. If he didn't leave now, he wouldn't go at all.

"I can't, Maddie," he said, his voice strained. "As much as I want to, I- I can't. Not tonight. My guilt over what I put you through at the party, and now looking at your beautiful body all cut and bruised because of me, I-I just can't. If I did, I'd be making a mockery of you ... of us, and what we've shared together. And when I entered this room tonight and saw the sheer exhaustion on your face from battling a fire you shouldn't have been exposed to in the first place, it – it shamed me to the quick. Then, when I begged you to forgive me and you merely shrugged me off, I realized that I didn't deserve your forgiveness now or ever. The way I see it, I'm no better than Alex."

Feeling the sting of rejection once again, Maddie clumsily grasped for the blanket with her good arm and covered her nakedness. "Are you through?" she asked dryly. Robert answered with a nod of his head.

She took in a deep breath and felt the bitterness of his betrayal taint her heart again. He still hadn't bothered to explain his peculiar relationship with Andrea, and she could only guess why. The truth would be too devasting. Maybe Andrea was like an illicit drug he couldn't leave alone. She felt her face contort in a hard frown. "You're absolutely right, Robert. You *are* no better than Alex...just smoother, more polished. Alex played the *poor me* card, blaming the universe for his bad luck when all the while he gloried in his *good* luck for latching on to me. I had a few bucks and some jewelry, and he sweet-talked me out of everything. *You*, on the other hand, stole my heart, then stomped on it like you would a bug. Not only are you sneaky and deceiving, you're the worst liar I have ever met."

"Liar!" Robert hissed. "I've *never* lied to you!"

Maddie became incensed. "The hell you didn't! What do *you* call a man who has sex on a beach one afternoon with a woman, and that very night goes back to that same exact spot and romances another woman? If that isn't being sneaky and deceitful, then I don't know what is. And to add insult to injury, you had the gall to come to me beforehand, all dolled up in your fancy dinner jacket, with the excuse that you had made plans before we met, and you couldn't get out of it!"

"I told you I tried, but–"

"Put a sock in it, Robert," she said scornfully. "I'm through battling with you. Now get out of here so I can finally get some sleep!"

The thread that held Robert's anger in check snapped. Maddie was right. It was time to end the fighting and false accusations. He had tried several times to get her to listen to him. He was not leaving her now until she did. Moving forward, he sat back down on the bed.

"Now what?" she hissed.

He took her uninjured hand in his. "I have something to say, and I don't want you to utter a word."

She started to open her mouth to object, but he put up a hand to silence her. "Just hear me out. Let me have my say, and then I'll leave you alone. All right?"

She stiffened, then relaxed a little and nodded begrudgingly.

"Okay," he said, sighing with a bit of relief. "I know nothing I can say or do right now is going to convince you that I am not the sneaky, underhanded cad you think I am, so I'm not even going there. Tomorrow morning, I'm going back to the rooming house to see if anything is salvageable, especially your purse and its contents. When I come back, I'll be bringing someone with me who will prove to you that I've never lied to you. *Never*! Everything will be explained in full detail, and I'll finally be exonerated."

He paused to let his words sink in. She eyed him

critically. "I don't expect you at this point to believe me or trust me, but just agree to give me the benefit of the doubt for the next twelve hours. Please." He thought he saw a flicker of acknowledgement in her eyes, and squeezed her hand reassuringly. "All I'm asking is that you trust me in this, and let me prove myself to you in the morning. Everything will become clear then. Please. Just nod your head and promise me you'll give me that."

Maddie closed her eyes and gave thought to what he had just said. She wouldn't have to keep torturing herself by going over and over the myriad conversations and events that had taken place since she'd been here to try and figure out where she stood with Robert. If what he said could be believed, tomorrow she'd have answers to all her questions, good or bad. All her worry and emotional pain could then be put to rest once and for all. She opened her eyes slowly and nodded her head.

"Wonderful!" Robert exclaimed, squeezing her hand. "Now, one last question."

Maddie pursed her lips. *What could he possibly want to know now?*

"Miss Madelyn Joan Price, will you marry me?"

Maddie felt her heart drop down to her stomach in sheer shock. Were her ears playing tricks on her? Why would Robert ask such a thing? What would he possibly have to gain by proposing marriage to her? Tears sprang to eyes, but she said nothing. Regardless of the fact that Robert had asked her not to say anything until he was done talking, she found herself at a loss for words. How could she agree to marry this man whom she loved but also mistrusted? Her heart told her he was a good and gentle, kind man, but her experience warned her to be wary, not to trust any man. All she could do was swallow painfully.

Robert waited, but Maddie said nothing. "Well?" he asked, sweat beading on his forehead. Then he remembered. "You can speak now."

The way Maddie looked at him, he wasn't sure her tears were from joy or sheer emotional pain. He felt his love and confidence curl up inside him like a shriveled leaf. Maybe he'd hurt her so badly with the Andy/Andrea thing, that he'd killed whatever feelings she'd had for him. He felt his stomach roll in protest. "Please, Maddie, say *something*!"

"Yes," she whimpered, tears streaming down her face. The word felt so right, being said in response to his proposal, but her mind screamed at her that she was making the same mistake she'd made with Alex – trusting blindly just because some man had offered the olive branch of marriage. "Yes," she said again, more emphatically, sobbing as Robert held her close.

"I love you, Maddie," he murmured near her ear. "No matter what's happened, no matter how terrible things seem right now, I want you to know that I really and truly do love you!"

Maddie let her tears fall uncontrolled and gradually relaxed against him, telling herself how wonderful everything would finally be, once tomorrow arrived and this mysterious stranger came back with Robert to vindicate him of any wrongdoing. She didn't know what peculiar truth he'd kept from her about Andrea, but good or bad, he wouldn't have proposed marriage to her if he didn't really mean it. He had no ulterior motive to marry her. How could he? She had absolutely nothing left to take, and he had no need of any material things she could offer. His love *had* to be genuine. It just had to be. And believing that much appeased her. She didn't see that there was a snowball's chance in hell that *anything* could go wrong from now on.

CHAPTER ELEVEN

---

*M*rs. O'Malley opened the door to Maddie's room at nine a.m. sharp just as she always did. Setting down a breakfast tray on top of the bureau, she automatically went and opened the French doors. She stood there a moment, drinking in the bright morning sun, then turned to wake Maddie up. To her surprise, Maddie was already awake, and smiling from ear to ear.

The housekeeper gave her an ominous look. "You grinning like Cheshire cat, just like Missah Kendall. How come? What big secret you not telling?"

Maddie acted coy. "What are you talking about?"

"Don't play dumb, Missy. Missah Kendall dance me around kitchen at seven o'clock this morning, singing like a bird. And you *know* Missah Kendall, he no carry tune from here to there. When I ask him why he so happy after horrible night, he just say, 'You see. It surprise.' Well, I no like surprise, make me nervous. So you better tell me truth if you want breakfast."

Beaming from ear to ear, Maddie blurted out, "Last night, Mr. Kendall asked me to marry him, and I said yes. Isn't it wonderful?"

At first, the housekeeper didn't react, which surprised Maddie, seeing how the older woman had been pushing them together since she first arrived. Maddie's smile quickly turned into a frown. "Aren't you happy about the news?"

"Of course I happy," she admitted. "I always know you two belong together right from start. I just surprise he ask you last night, that all."

The housekeeper's statement churned in Maddie's stomach, and she bolted upright. "Why? Did something happen after I left the party?" Then it quickly donned on her. Robert must have gone into a jealous rage over his brother's attention to Andrea. If so, why did he propose to her? Was Robert one of those possessive jerks who wanted every woman for himself?

"Answer me, Mrs. O'Malley," she snapped. "Now! I want to know why you're surprised Mr. Kendall proposed last night. I don't like surprises either, and Robert will be home soon. So tell me what happened."

The older woman dropped down on Maddie's vanity chair. Keeping her eyes lowered, she said, "I surprise he ask you last night because ... because he say he want to ask you at picnic on beach. But you take off and I think I never see you again. Then, all hell break loose when Missah Kendall see his brother David with red-hair hussy. He grabbed them both by their arms and drag them into the foyer. I getting clean glasses at bar when I hear Missah Kendall say to Andrea something like, 'Get you sorry ass outa here right now! This game–' only he don't say 'game', he say some other word like 'shrade' '–it go on long enough.' And he say Andrea destroy his relationship with you, and he be damn if he let hussy come between him and brother. Then he tell hussy to get out, and he tell David something in his ear I don't hear. But whatever he say, it make David almost sick, and he leave right away. Then party seem like it end and everybody leave, 'cause they know Missah Kendall pretty upset. We start clean up, then scanner go off about fire in Plymouth. He call for Caesar and then take off. And, that all I know. Anyhow, I real glad you and Missah Kendall make up, 'cause when *he* not happy, *nobody* happy."

She got up from the chair and took the breakfast tray over to Maddie. "You eat now. When you done, I give you nice sponge bath. By then, Missah Kendall be back and I go shop for you." She took out a small pad of paper and a pen from her apron pocket and handed it to Maddie. "You write sizes for clothes and shoes. I look for good, thick slippers too."

Maddie was so hungry, she practically wolfed down her French toast and scrambled eggs, stopping just long enough to jot down the information needed, then handed back the paper and pen to the Mrs. O'Malley.

"This is sooooo delicious," Maddie said between bites. "Keep feeding me meals like this every day, and I'll shoot up to two hundred pounds in no time."

Laughing, the housekeeper quipped, "Then I better get larger sizes than what you wrote. You eat my meals for a week."

"Have mercy," Maddie giggled as she sipped the last of her coffee. When she was through, Mrs. O'Malley gave her a warm sponge bath, then checked the bruises on her arm, shoulder and feet. "How Missy feel this morning?" the older woman asked as she applied a fresh coating of ointment on Maddie's cuts.

"Real sore," Maddie answered, "now that the shot the doctor gave me has worn off."

Mrs. O'Malley frowned. "Aspirin strongest pain medicine we keep in the house. Missah Kendall a fanatic about pills. He never take any, even when he get awful headache. He just go to his room, take hot shower, and go to bed." She had returned to the bathroom to clean up.

"Mrs. O'Malley, could you please brush my hair?" Maddie called after her. "I don't want Robert to see me looking like a witch with my hair all twisted and matted."

* * * * *

Maddie and Mei-Lin were engaged in small talk when Robert entered the room. "Good morning, ladies," he chimed, setting several boxes and bags down on the floor. "And how is our patient feeling this morning?" he asked, stepping to the bed where he placed a light kiss on Maddie's lips.

"Couldn't be better," she answered, gazing lovingly up at him.

"Good to hear it," he replied.

By this time, Mrs. O'Malley was at the bedroom door. "Now you here, Missah K, I go shopping for Maddie. She gave me list. Long list. I gone awhile."

She was just about to close the door behind her when Robert called out, "Mei-Lin! Take my credit card and get her everything she wants – and some pretty things she didn't put on the list. Just have the stores charge them to me." He handed the card to Mei-Lin, who took it graciously, gave them both a nod of goodbye, then shut the door.

Robert couldn't wait for her to leave. He settled himself down on the side of the bed and gently took Maddie in his arms. He nestled his face in the side of her neck, taking in the clean, delicious smell of soap and water. He never cared for the smell of perfume, no matter how expensive it was.

He turned her face to the side and took her mouth, needing her taste, her touch, to reassure himself that they were really okay. He had come incredibly close to losing her. Now, with his mouth fused to hers, he realized just how close, and he vowed by all that was holy, he'd never let anything take her away from him again. Just the thought of it made his insides quiver and his heart beat so rapidly that he was sure Maddie could feel it through the thin pajama top she wore.

Cupping his face in her hands, Maddie released her lips from his and said anxiously, "Robert, you're shaking. What's wrong?" For the first time since they met, Maddie saw him become emotionally unnerved, and it frightened her.

Robert answered her by reaching down into one of the bags. His hand shook as he removed the morning's newspaper. Unfolding it, he placed it on Maddie's lap. "Take a look at this," he said, pointing to the front page headlines. Maddie's eyes widened as she read the boldly printed words – *Woman Saves Boarding House Residents From Deadly Fire.* Below the headlines was a giant picture of her sitting on the curb giving an infant CPR. Beneath the picture was the caption, *Boarding House Heroine Saves Life Of Dying Infant* along with a complete story which included her full name and occupation, stating that she was the secretary to the renowned playwright, Robert Kendall of Bourne, Massachusetts.

After she read the complete article, Maddie looked over at Robert, whose eyes were brimming with tears. He didn't look at her but said in a voice that was low and raspy, "I can't tell you how proud I am of you. You risked your own life to save the lives of all those people, especially the baby's. You were more than courageous, you were–"

"I was there," she cut in, her voice calm and serene. "I did what I had to do. You would have done the same thing."

"Perhaps," he said. "But what breaks my heart is knowing that you shouldn't have been there to begin with. You should have been at the party with me. And you would've been if I had come clean with you right from the start about Andrea."

She looked at him, and a strange tender look entered her pale blue eyes. "Maybe so. But I also believe in Divine Intervention. If I hadn't gone back to the rooming house, I wouldn't have been there to save those people, especially the child. Perhaps, someone else would've saved them. I'll never know. But it's over and done with, Robert. Let it go. I'm here, and I'm safe, and all those people are safe, too." She gave him a quick peck on the cheek. "Now, show me what's in those boxes and bags."

The first item he showed her was a gorgeous blue satin pajama set with a long matching robe that tied at the waist. Lighter blue hand-sewn appliqués circled the hem of the pajama top and the sleeves of both the pajamas and the robe. The feel of the material was luxurious. Maddie decided she would wear it that afternoon when Robert entertained his guest.

Each box he opened contained an outfit more beautiful than the last. There were pastel peignoirs, sweaters, slacks, blouses and some sexy-laced bras and panties.

"You naughty boy," Maddie squealed while laughing and rubbing the soft lingerie between her fingers. She began to fold each item carefully when Robert stopped her. His eyes were sad, and a deep frown creased his brow. "I went back to the rooming house," he said quietly. "What a mess. Everything was either burned or ruined by the water. Nothing was salvageable. Not even your purse. While you're off your feet this week, I'll do my best to replace the important things like your driver's license, and whatever else you need."

"Thank you for everything you've done and all you're still doing. I really do appreciate it," she said lovingly.

"My pleasure," he answered, pulling her close to him.

"Ouch!" she exclaimed when her tender breast collided with the pocket of his jeans jacket.

"Sorry about that," he apologized, reaching inside for its contents. "You must have hit this." He opened his hand and revealed a small white leather box. "Open it."

Maddie's hands shook as she slowly opened the box, only to discover it contained another box. She gave him a sly look. When she opened the last box she could do nothing but gasp and cry at the same time.

"Like it?" he asked, his face beaming.

"Like it? Oh, Robert, it's magnificent! It must have cost you a fortune!"

"You're worth every penny," he said, as he took the ring from the box and slid it onto her finger. The white gold band sported a three-carat marquis diamond surrounded by baguettes that created a dazzling display. Tears of happiness ran down her cheeks as she brought Robert's mouth down to meet hers. Ah, the taste of her. There was the heated sweetness of her mouth. He sampled it, then tasted again more deeply, making love to her with his tongue. Then there was the fragrant hollow of her throat and the fresh clean taste of her breasts. He lingered there until her fingers were twisting in the covers, and her hips were lifting against him.

Her belly was soft and cool against his lips. Her tight little navel invited exploration, and he circled it with his tongue. Her hands moved into his hair and tightly pressed against his head as he moved downward, parting her thighs and draping them over his shoulders.

She breathed hard, her body twisting and straining. He held her hips and loved her, not stopping until she heaved upward and cried out as the waves of completion overtook her.

Maddie felt drained. She lay still as Robert knelt between her legs and tore at his clothes, throwing them aside. She could barely open her eyes as he positioned himself and then invaded her with a slow, heavy thrust that carried him into her to the hilt. As before, she was faintly startled by the overwhelming sense of fullness as she adjusted herself to him.

His full weight was on her, pressing her downward. There was nothing gentlemanly about him now, only the need to enter her as deeply as possible, to carry the embrace to the fullest so that there was no part of her that didn't feel his possession. There was a savagery in him that needed to be appeased, a hunger that needed to be fed. She was helpless to do anything but lie there and accept him, feeling her passion rising again with his until they both exploded in ecstasy.

* * * * *

Robert was busy hanging Maddie's new outfits in the closet when Mrs. O'Malley entered the room, laden with her own boxes and packages. It was obvious by the deep circles under her eyes and the drawn look on her face that she was exhausted.

"Let me take those," Robert urged, as the housekeeper dropped down onto the vanity chair. Maddie felt bad for the woman. "You shouldn't have bought so many items," she said. "I'm not going anywhere, and Robert went shopping for me as well." She shimmied herself down to the bottom of the bed, and extending her hand said, "Look at the beautiful engagement ring Robert just gave me. Isn't it gorgeous?"

Mrs. O'Malley leaned forward and took Maddie's hand in hers. Eying the exquisite diamond, the housekeeper gave Robert an ominous look. "This mean I got to take a cut in pay?"

Robert roared with laughter. "Only for about six months."

Tears filled the older woman's eyes. When she spoke, it was evident her words came from her heart. "I so happy for both of you. And I wish you long happiness all you life. God bless you." Without a warning, Robert gathered his housekeeper up into his arms and began twirling her around the room. The woman cried out in protest, "You not gonna dance with me again, Missah K! I still pooped from this morning, and you step on my feet like big ox!" she teased.

The joy and happiness that now filled the room touched Maddie's heart to the point she thought she would burst. It was so hard to believe that less than twenty-four hours ago she was hurting so badly, she had to run away to escape the pain of it.

Robert put the woman back down on her feet, and like an inquisitive child, he began searching through the new set of boxes and bags. Withdrawing a beautifully wrapped package, Robert gave Maddie a wicked wink as he unwrapped it, noting that it came from the most exquisite and expensive boutique in town.

"That little number for you, Missah K," Mrs. O'Malley pointed out as Robert held up a see-through white teddy, complete with a short matching robe and slippers.

Maddie blushed when Robert ogled the sexy nightie. Their thoughts collided, and again the room filled with laughter.

Putting the remaining packages in a corner, Mrs. O'Malley announced she was going to fix them a light lunch, as Robert's guest would be arriving shortly.

"Thank you, my friend," Robert called out to her as she closed the bedroom door behind her.

* * * * *

An hour later, Maddie was sitting on a chaise longue out on the veranda. Robert had dressed her in the blue pajama set, robe and slippers, and had brushed her hair until it fell in soft waves over her shoulders and down her back. The makeup Mrs. O'Malley had selected for her was perfect. When she was through with her grooming, it was impossible to detect that Maddie had braved a raging fire the night before.

The couple had just finished their lunch when Mrs.

O'Malley stepped out onto the veranda with a tray of freshly brewed coffee and homemade pastries. In a tiny cup was the antibiotic the doctor had prescribed the night before. "Down the hatch, Missy," the housekeeper said, making sure Maddie took the capsule. As she was leaving, she informed Robert that his guest was pulling into the driveway.

"Thank you, Mei-Lin. Send him right up."

In a matter of minutes the two men were shaking hands in the veranda's doorway. The gentleman's back was to Maddie, so she couldn't see his face. What she did see was a man, very much on the slim side with hair as blonde as hers, and a voice quite deep, but soft and pleasant on the ears.

"Sweetheart, I'd like you to meet my best friend, Andy."

The man turned, and extending his hand to her, looked deeply into her eyes. "Pleasure to finally meet you, Miss Price," he said keeping his green eyes locked with hers.

"Same here," she uttered, offering him a pleasant smile. Was it her imagination, or had she met him somewhere before? Wracking her subconscious, she tried to ascertain where and when she might have run into him. She thought it odd that the man sitting before her was more than handsome. He could be regarded as beautiful.

"Have you and Robert been friends for a long time?" she asked, inquisitively.

"Yes, ma'am, we have," he answered.

"That's strange," Maddie quipped. "I've been staying here as Mr. Kendall's guest and employee for a while now. How come we've never met?"

Andy flashed her a wide smile. "Oh, we've met.

Several times, in fact."

That's when it hit Maddie. Robert could tell she had figured it out and was about to explode with anger, so he got up from his seat and went to her side, making sure she didn't get to her feet.

"Have I gone completely insane, Robert, or is your friend Andy really *Andrea*?" she asked incredulously.

"No, Maddie," Robert stated, "you haven't gone insane. Andy and Andrea *are* the same person. We tried to tell you–"

"Let me explain it, Robert," Andy cut in. "I feel that I should be the one to set the record straight, seeing that I'm basically the cause for all the trouble and pain Maddie's endured since she came here."

He filled his cup with coffee, took a sip, then said on a deep sigh, "A few months back, Robert put out what's called a cattle call, because he needed a character actor for the play he's writing now. I happen to be a character actor, and wanted desperately to be a part of his production. Now, the part calls for the actor to play a dual role, one a man and the other a woman, like in the film *Victor/Victoria*. I knew I could pull it off, but Robert wasn't so sure. I told Robert that if he gave me the part I would only appear in public as his *friend* Andrea. Nobody – not even Mrs. O'Malley was to know my real identity. As luck would have it, nobody questioned my gender."

Maddie listened to him in silence, her face expressionless. But inside, she wanted to tear his heart out. His charade had served him well, but it had practically destroyed the relationship between herself and Robert, not once but twice – and the last time had nearly cost her her life. She turned her head and looked up at Robert, fire blazing in her eyes. That he had been a party to this deception was unforgivable. She took her gaze from Robert to stare at the diamond whose sparkle practically blinded her in the early afternoon sun, then returned to Andy, who was still speaking.

"...and I'm afraid it was my fault that you saw Robert and me on the beach that night. He wanted no part of it, but I insisted we test you. Well, that little scene nearly cost me the part and would've destroyed our friendship if I hadn't promised to tell you the truth myself in the morning. I came over, but you wouldn't stay and hear us out.

"I had no idea that Robert's brother was in the dark about me. All I can say is that I ... I got caught up in the attention I was getting from all the men, which solidified my belief that not only would an audience believe I was a woman, but that I had an outstanding chance of winning a Tony for my performance. But again, I never got the chance to tell you. You thought Robert was acting jealous over David's attention to me, which was not the case. David believed I was a woman and – and Robert just wanted to spare his brother the embarrassment of discovering I was a man."

Maddie turned to Robert, and she could tell by his stiff demeanor that he was fast losing control. He jammed his hands into the pockets of his jeans and began to pace back and forth between her and Andy.

"Say what you have to say before you explode, Robert," she said dryly. He came and squatted at the foot of the chaise and spoke in an iron-hard voice. "Forget everything Andy just told you, Maddie. I'm the bad guy here. I had the chance last night before the party to explain everything to you, but I put it off, thinking that after all the attempts I'd made to try and convince you nothing was going on, you wouldn't believe me. I thought that if, at the party, both Andy and I together told you what was behind all the secrecy, we'd all have a good laugh over it – once you got over being angry with me. Only this whole thing backfired on me, and you paid the consequences. Now that you know the truth, I wouldn't blame you if you called off our engagement and never wanted to see me again."

"And give up this gorgeous diamond ring?" Maddie exclaimed. "Not on your life!" The three of them chuckled for a moment, then Maddie announced she had something to say. "I believe everybody deserves a second chance in life. I've certainly made my share of mistakes and bad judgments. And as for you, Andy, I know what it feels like to want something so bad you could taste it. You actually become blindsided by your desire to get what you want, so I really can't fault you for what you did. And I have to admit, you make one helluva good looking broad."

Andy stood up and went to Maddie. He gave her a giant hug and said, "Don't ever doubt Robert's love for you. He's a good man, and I know he'll make you happy for the rest of your life."

* * * * *

Three weeks went by, and Maddie was back to her old self again. Andy became a frequent guest, as *Andy* and not Andrea. Mrs. O'Malley went back to her routine, and even Caesar loved to lie down at Maddie's feet as she worked on Robert's play.

She was in Robert's office with him one cold and rainy morning when Mrs. O'Malley stuck her head in the doorway and announced that Maddie had a visitor. Wondering who it could possibly be, she stepped out into the foyer.

"Hello there, gorgeous," the familiar voice hummed.

Fearing she was about to faint, Maddie stepped back and leaned against the wall for support. "What in God's name are *you* doing here?" she asked, looking at Alex as though she were seeing a ghost.

"I came to take you back with me where you belong," he said, his eyes scanning the surroundings.

Maddie looked at him long and hard. He still had his rugged good looks; dazzling smile; and charm that could melt the coldest heart. Whatever it was about him that had attracted her to him in the first place came rushing to the surface, but somehow didn't have the same effect on her anymore. "How did you find me?"

He pulled out a newspaper from inside his leather jacket. "From the story here in this paper. I picked it up at a newsstand in Paris. Seems you're quite the heroine. Not surprising. You were always *my* heroine."

"Sure I was," Maddie hissed sarcastically. "I was also your money machine, the proceeds from which I'm sure you've squandered away by now."

"That's not fair, Maddie," Alex practically crooned. "I had to come back for you. You're my unforgettable love. Don't you remember? Our song – *Unforgettable*?"

"Unfortunately, I do. Now turn your sorry ass around and get lost." With that, Maddie slammed the door in his face.

"What's going on out here?" Robert asked inquisitively as he came out of the office.

"Nothing, honey," she answered. "Just some *totally*

forgettable con man trying to sell stuff we neither want nor need."

Robert circled his arm around Maddie's shoulders. She didn't bother to look back as she relaxed in his caress and walked with him down the hallway. "We have everything we need, right here."

~Coming Soon Preview~

Dark Crescendo

Carlton Reed lunged at Nick Jordan. Grabbing him by the shirt collar, he pulled him forward and bellowed, "What kind of a man seduces a woman two weeks after her husband's death? And in a public restaurant, yet!"

"It wasn't like that at all, Father," Joanna broke in. "Nick didn't force himself on me. I went to him willingly. In fact, Nick came here to ask me to marry him, and I have accepted."

"Have you taken leave of your senses, child?" Carlton asked disbelievingly.

"For the love of God, Father, will you stop regarding me as a child? I am an adult, and I thought I'd made that point abundantly clear to you last night, or have you seen fit–"

"I haven't forgotten last night," he snapped back. "But I sure in hell didn't interpret your bid for freedom as a license to behave like a common trollop, especially with the likes of a Nick Jordan! This time you've scraped the bottom of the barrel, Joanna, and it shames me to discover the depths to which you will sink to, all in the name of love!"

~About the Author~

LUCILLE NAROIAN

 A resident of northern Massachusetts and the mother of a grown son, Lucille Naroian has held a variety of job positions, including cosmetologist, chiropractor's assistant, pharmacy technician, and administrator in the stock market. In addition to indulging her love of writing, Lucille is an award-winning portrait artist and enjoys tending her aquarium of tropical fish.

Lucille's debut novel, **Talk of the Town**, is a spicy and humorous romance. **Unforgettable** is her second published novel, with **Dark Crescendo** coming soon. Look for Lucille's books at Amazon and other popular book retailers.

To learn more about Lucille and her books, please visit her web site at...

www.LucilleNaroian.webs.com

Lucille enjoys hearing from readers and can be contacted by visiting Penumbra Publishing's web site at...

www.PenumbraPublishing.com